He had earned his gold Detective's shield the hard way, night school and in a uniform. Now the tall man who carried a weapon that was not standard, but could shoot through a car door, had a record of closing more cases with some of the toughest criminals on the streets.

The Night Watcher

ISBN: 978-1-4874-4156-2
Cover art by SudaGraphics Inc

Published by eXtasy Books Inc

Look for us online at:
www.eXtasybooks.com

The Night Watcher

By

M. Garnet

Dedication

Sometime the muse in me needs a nudge. Then my daughter, who is a great IT artist, draws me to her Etsy site and there it is. A cover she has created for sale to convince customers she can help them produce an eye catching cover for their book. But one on the ad page had a story in it for me, so I stole it and here it is.

Covers do sell books. Her site at Etsy is:

https://www.etsy.com/search?q=sudaGraphics&ref=search_bar
Remember to leave a comment about this book wherever you got it.
Thanks so much.
www.mgarnet.com

CHAPTER ONE

It would be dawn soon and this world would change. Like part of the shadows, a drunken man stumbled across too much debris in the side street. The high street lights only gave a hazy glow to the cluttered sidewalk. He was fumbling in his pocket for his phone, with his puddled attention anywhere but where he was walking, when he fell flat over a low barrier on the pavement.

Rolling over with a groan as he felt the pain in one knee, he came face to face with a woman who looked in worse shape than him. Pushing himself away from the pale face, he worked to stand up, but accidently placed a hand on the lady. She felt cold and didn't move.

"Damn," he muttered, sick from his own breath. This woman was dead. Again, he worked to bring out the phone and punched in the 911. All he could do now was move over and lean against a wall.

Although the sirens could be heard in the distance, the drunk leaning on the wall was surprised when another man appeared out of the shadows and approached the death scene.

"Stay back. I've called the cops." The drunk held up his phone as if it were a weapon.

The man with a light grey fedora low over his eyes, pulled his jacket back and flashed a badge attached to his belt. Then he began to pull on some latex gloves and knelt down next to the head of the lovely dead lady.

The drunk took a few steps sideways, glad for the wall for

support. He really wanted to get away from this whole mad spectacle. He was looking at a beautiful dead woman and a cop who had appeared out of nowhere as if by magic. He thought he was going to be sick.

"Walk out to the corner to heave. We don't want the crime scene disturbed."

The drunk was surprised at the low order from the man down on his heels. But he understood the strange cop's order and holding on with one hand move to the end of the building before everything in his stomach hit his shoes. Even with all the unusual smells in this dark neighborhood, his vomit made him heave again.

The glare of flashing red and blue lights made him close his eyes and wish he could close his ears from the loud sirens. There was more than one cop car with bright headlights on him and now down the side narrow street.

From the cars poured a number of people in the dark blue uniforms, some with weapons in their hands. A couple grabbed the drunk and others worked in alert motions toward the body. At that point the man in the grey fedora stood up and pulled his coat back again to show his gold shield.

"I was in the area and heard the 911 call. We need a Supervisor and a Crime Scene Unit. She has been dead for a long time and she was not killed here." He spoke as he looked down at the body.

A couple of the uniforms approached and turned bright flashlights on to highlight the lady. One of them reached down, but the detective stopped him.

"Put gloves on. Don't contaminate the crime scene." Now he pulled out his own flash and began to look at the body's feet and the area of the sidewalk.

The contrite uniform stood up and stepped back. "I need some gloves to check for body temperature."

"What, idiot," another uniform standing behind him spoke

in a low voice. "You think she is still alive with her head bent like that? I'm putting thru the calls." With that the smarter cop stepped away and spoke into his mic on his shoulder.

His buddy who was watching the detective work the sidewalk, turned and nudged his friend when he was done on the mic call. "Who is the detective that got here before we did?"

"Ah, he is a legend." The second guy pulled his friend back away from the tableau. "That is Detective Damian Walker. It is whispered that he lives on these streets at night. Always seems to get to a crime scene before anyone else. He's a real wild card." The uniform tapped his weapon that was back in its holster. "His last two partners were killed on the job, so now no one will work with him."

The first guy turned and looked in the brightness of the headlights at his buddy. "Good story but you are full of shit. I'm going back to the car for my coffee."

Dawn did bring a different picture to this particular cross street. The flashing lights of the cop cars were everywhere as uniforms were going from door to door and upstairs to question individuals for information. A large Crime Scene Unit truck was now up front and in center position with all the yellow tape marking off a large area on both ends of the street where the body was covered by a sheet. Over the body was a portable tent on metal legs to prevent any moisture from the dawn's mist to settle on the area.

Only two people were near the body and they were covered from head to toe in light blue protective clothing. On the back of the open doors of the Unit's truck sat the detective and the supervisor.

The supervisor held out a fingerprint scanner. "We got a hit."

The detective nodded and watched as she turned and opened a portable computer on the floor of the truck. It didn't take her long to get on line with the latest equipment that the police department had supplied their staff. It actually took her longer to go through the internal system to trace for information on the name that had come up on the fingerprint ID. The detective sat quietly as the woman worked, looking out at the CSI people working.

"Ah, damn," the Supervisor swore. "She is Caroline Becker, a third year student at Community College. What is she doing dressed like a hooker. The whore house is right around the corner from this spot."

"They will find she has been redressed. She wasn't a pro. It was made to look that way." The Detective pointed at something one of the CSI guys was examining. The woman's skirt was buttoned and zippered on the wrong side. Women's clothes were manufactured that if they closed on a side, it will always be on the left. Someone had redressed the dead body.

"This is the third one in fourteen nights." The Supervisor had a split screen up and there were pictures of two other women laid out on streets in similar poses as the girl in front of them. "We have a serial killer."

"I'm going back to HQ and start on my report. I'll send everything to you." The Detective slowly left the scene, passing the corner. Usually at this time of the morning the special door of one business was closed up tight. Instead, it was open and a woman in a long silk wrap was standing in it, watching all the activity.

"Hey, Damian," the woman called out. "Was it one of ours?"

Looking over at the working woman in her loose robe, the Detective shook his head. "Not this time, Rosy. Take care."

Moving on past the clog of official vehicles, the tall slender man walked slowly on down the sidewalk, looking at the watchers. Sometimes a killer liked to stay around and watch the activity the dead body caused. But this time the Detective doubted that the killer was present. He had a hunch the perpetrator was too smart.

Several blocks away he approached his car. The low slung dark Charger with tinted windows came from the back of the police station's garage where apprehended and unclaimed vehicles were temporarily stored. Detectives often could obtain vehicles from the garage if needed and if the cars were not involved in legal cases. What Damian liked about this muscle car was that when the strong engine was running, it didn't roar, it purred. No one had made the mistake of putting the loud exhausts onto the monster.

The only changes he had made to Detroit's pride was pop up lights in the back windows and behind the front grill. Nothing showed until he hit the right buttons and then he got a siren and the red and blue lights to stop anyone. If someone was stupid enough to run, this car could take them down easily. Damian loved the low vehicle.

Pulling in behind the two story police station that took up most of the city block. In back of the large garage for parking on one side and the storage area for work for the mechanics. The area for the apprehended and held vehicles was behind on a separate block inside a high wire fence.

Parking in a Reserved place for officers higher in rank than Detectives, he made his way into the back door and through the well lit cubbies for the cops that deserved a place for their own work places. His was over one aisle and down a couple of slots. There was an empty place next to him since he did not have a partner, but the guy on the other side slid out and nodded.

"Hey Walker, another busy night, huh?" The guy was a young detective, but did a reasonable job. Damian liked the young man. Under the right circumstances the kid would make a good detective. He was teamed up with a guy who was near retirement and didn't want to do anything but punch his time card. The older detective never came into the office this early, but the kid showed up in hopes of something interesting falling their way.

"Yeah," Damian nodded as he slid down into the comfortable chair and brought up the screen on the desk computer. "I have a full report to fill in before I fall asleep. If I fall out of this chair, come over here and kick me."

The kid laughed but had the sense to leave the busy man alone as he began to bring up standard forms to fill. It would be a long morning.

It was a longer morning for a tired EMT workers who were returning to their apartment together after a longer than usual night on their job. He was the driver of the ambulance with a trained medical assistant in the front and she was a trained medical assistant that always rode in the back.

He was a large handsome muscular guy that got a lot of attraction from the females and usually had to handle anything that required pushing or pulling. She was a small but compact woman who could still handle any wheel chair or the rolling transport beds from their vehicle. The third man was a young guy on the small side and tended to be shy, but did follow orders from both of the other. They separated at the EMT station and the kid took a bus home while the pair took their small sedan to the apartment they shared.

As they entered the downstair basement apartment, she was the one who gave directions. "You go ahead and straighten up the bedroom. I will clean up the bathroom. I'll be a while because the last one needed a lot of work."

He dumped his heavy jacked over a hook at the door and started down the hallway. "You sure you want me to put everything away? We can have some fun of our own later." There was almost a sexy question in his voice.

"Don't tempt me." She answered with a laugh. "You know

I love it when you clamp those ties to my wrists. But I think I will be tired after I am done. Maybe tomorrow night we will let you be a Dom." She hummed as she left him to begin to pull cleaning tools from a cabinet. She had not even pulled her jacket or boots off.

Stopping in the door of the bathroom, she looked at all the make-up and nail polish that was still out in kits standing on the floor. With a sigh, she set the bucket full of tools and mop down, went back to the entry and took off her jacket and boots. Now it was time to get serious and clean the bathroom. Men never understood how important it was to have a clean bathroom.

CHAPTER TWO

At last Damian got to his apartment. Some would be shocked to visit this one room where the Detective lived, but it suited him. It was one large room with an equally large bathroom off to one side. One whole wall was cabinets from the high ceiling to the floor with an inset work space. Some of the cabinets had dial pads for a lock to open. On another wall was a built-in kitchen, everything in one place and narrow with fridge and stove and work area and open areas showing plates and pans and utensils.

Best of all, thought Damian, on the outside wall that was windows waist high stood a wide king size bed. It was all pillows and heavy duvets with no direct head or foot. Except for the bed the room and bathroom were extremely neat.

Pulling off his cap he nudged a handle less cabinet and it popped open. He hung the hat and took off his coat to put it on a large wooden hanger inside the same long cabinet. By the time he came out of the bathroom he was stripped down in comfortable loose pants. He hit a button on the wall near his bed and there was a loud banging as shutters slammed down over the windows and the room was in darkness.

It was the next midnight when the Detective was down in the basement of HQ. It was where the morgue was located and with no windows and all the bright lights, there was no day or night in this place. Due to the crime in this bustling city, the morgue had three shifts running all the time, with competent aides and good Pathologists heading up the staffs.

Now Damian was on first names with the Doctor in charge

of the final shift as they both worked the eleven pm to seven am. That was the official time, but both often worked longer hours if cases piled up.

"Hey Jean," the Detective spoke as he made his way through the aisle of bodies.

"Welcome Damion, I figured this lady was yours. You are too early, but I promise I will stay and look her over. They put her aside because they were swamped in here yesterday due to a house fire." The Pathologist didn't look up as she was doing something that he didn't want to know about. "This is awfully familiar."

"Damn. I thought the same thing when I saw her on the curb. Someone put on her make up and dressed her." Damion leaned against another tall table in the cold room and watched his friend work. This was not an area he enjoyed. It was not his environment, not because of the dead bodies, but because he was a person of the dark. He needed to be out right now on the dark streets seeking the night crawlers who used the lack of light to prey on others.

"Damian," the doctor talked as she stepped back and raised her face shield. "This killer has real deep problems. Please be careful."

"Always am, Jean. Send me a copy of the report when you're done. Thanks." The Detective left to go up the stairs and out into the dark to find his car with a notice on the windshield. He knew what it was. It was a warning about parking in wrong place. As the car purred into action, he headed back to the crime scene for one more look.

For the night people, one o'clock was the right time for partying and hunting for hidden poker games and whores. All of it was easy to find in this part of the busy city. Actually, it was available in most parts of the city as overgrowth, poverty and lack of law made it the rule for the streets. This great metropolis that had once been a magnificent lady now had stained skirts. This Detective was down here in the dirt and recognized all the problems.

There was a tattered yellow police ribbon across the side street with one black and white parked in front to block it off. The doors of the cop car were open and one uniform leaned against the hood. Walker wondered where the guy's partner was, off or coffee or in talking to the whores. The girls in the building on the corner with no outside lights or marker or name except for the number on the wall beside the door that was wide open. The red and orange bright lights made long streaks out onto the dirty sidewalk and was better advertisement than any sign.

Getting out with his two cup of coffee that he had picked up at the local drive thru, he usually drank both himself. But it never hurt to make a friend among the guys who were on the street as much as him.

"Did they leave you out here by yourself tonight?" The Detective held out the coffee and the cop seemed surprised. Most people with the gold shield always acted aloof around the uniforms. Damian remembered back to his time actually walking a beat.

"Thanks." The surprised guy popped the small spot on top and took a sample of the hot liquid. "With the recent cut backs, there is only one to a car."

They sat against the car and watched people cross the street to avoid the cops and the danger of the yellow tape. Still, everyone was interested and gawked at the two men drinking their favorite coffee from large paper cups with a logo everyone could recognize.

"I'm going to take one more look at the scene. I won't get close to interfere with anything CSI might come back for tomorrow."

"Hey, no problem. Thanks for the joe." The cop tipped his cup.

Walking around to the back of the cop car, Damian dumped the last of his coffee and looked up to see a lady's silhouette in the special doorway. Bending over, he pushed his cup down the curb's drain and then stood and tipped his hat at the lady.

"Early in the mornin' and its freebees for cops, Detective." The woman spoke with a laugh. She turned and flipped up her skirt to show him a bare bottom. He shook his head, sorry to miss out on a nice invitation, but he had something else on his mind.

Walking down the sidewalk on the opposite side in the dim glow of the overhead street lights, he had a vision of the other two sites. Scenes where two pretty young women had been left on display after being killed somewhere else. They all had been dressed in old clothes, probably picked up at a Salvation Station somewhere. They were chosen to make the girls look like sluts, skirts too tight and short, no panties, lace bras and low-cut blouses. The heels would have been the type too high to walk in very far and their nails painted bright red.

The makeup on their faces had been done after they were dead and was too much. Heavy red lipstick, cheeks too much blush and eyes painted black with lashes colored dark. Someone wanted the cops to think this was just another dead whore, but the investigation soon began to prove something different about each of these women. There had been restraint marks on wrists and ankles, but they were the type used with wide bracelets covered in fur. These murders had been done by someone who was ready for the act. Yet it had only started three weeks ago. Why had the killer waited so long for his first kill?

In the distance, he heard a siren passing through the area. It was an EMT truck as they had a slightly higher sound than those on the vehicles of the police. It was another busy night in the dark of this city. Deciding he had found nothing more here, he returned to his car to cruise around and watch the eternally busy dim streets with lights from some bars.

Damian thought about these women, normal and reasonably nice. They were introduced to BDMS in not a nice way. No one taught them the stop or escape word. He had experimented with the MS world at the request of a female friend. He felt he got no more pleasure having a woman in chains than he did one who was smiling up at him in a soft bed.

Hearing a call for detectives in the area of Fourteenth and Maple made him look up at his location. He was cruising on Fourteenth. He hit the mic on the dashboard.

"This is Officer 2155. I will answer the 316 call." He heard the acknowledge and turned on the lights and siren that were hidden in his low car and moved around the slow moving traffic. He pulled up close behind several black and whites with their lights flashing blue and red against the walls of the local businesses. He shut everything off on his car and got out. He left his hat and coat in the car. This allowed the gold badge on his belt to be prominent. His special gun was in a holster in the middle of his back with the unusual extra sets of clips in leather pockets in back on the belt also. It was a different kind of set up, but no one made a comment of what detectives chose to wear their weapons.

As Damian walked into the crowd of uniforms and people in cuffs and some on the ground, a uniform turned and walked over to him.

"Detective. We got a mess. A store owner shot a couple of kids he says was trying to rob him. But the kids claim it isn't true." The cop pointed over to where there were four normal hoodies being held in cuffs and arguing with the uniforms. Separated from them was an older man in an apron, that a couple of uniforms was taking down information.

Looking around, he was pleased that the uniforms had everything on the outside under control. They had the kids off to the side yet under control so that they couldn't run. As he watched they were putting the rough kids into different cars so that they would not be talking to each other.

"You guys are doing a good job. Keep the kids apart and put in a call for a Supervisor, since we have someone down inside." As the Detective was talking, he heard the distant sound of an EMT Unit that would soon be at the location. He decided he wanted to get inside and look at the scene before the emergency team took over and didn't let anyone near the bodies.

The unform that had met him, followed Damian as he walked around everyone and past the upset store owner.

"He claims one of them had a gun. We have searched them all and haven't found a gun. Over there you can see all the knives we pulled off of them." The uniform pointed to a hood of a black and white that was littered with knives and small plastic envelopes of what was probably some type of dope.

Inside and down one aisle full of dumped boxes of food, a body was sprawled out and leaking blood. Damian knew he didn't have to get close to know the kid was gone. But he heard a noise in the next row and the uniform also motioned.

"Damn," the uniform spoke as he moved carefully, trying to not disturb anything. "I hope they don't charge that old guy."

The boy was propped up against a shelf and was holding his stomach. Actually, from where the Detective stopped to look, it didn't seem as if the rough kid had been hit in a serious manner.

"Get me some help." The kid looked up and met their eyes. His face was half hidden by the standard hood from his sweatshirt, but what Damian could see was Hispanic. "That fucker shot me for no reason. Get me some fucking help."

Looking around and up at the ceiling, the Detective spied something important.

Chapter Three

"Hey, did any of you guys look at the camera reruns?"

"Have to be honest, Detective," the uniform was a good guy and now seemed a bit embarrassed. "We have had our hands full corralling the wild boys. Some of our guys had to chase these kids down the back alley."

Remembering his own time in the uniform and unlike a lot of Detectives who got testy along with the gold, Damian reached out to the man. He put his hand on the guy's shoulder.

"No problem. You guys did good by catching everyone and separating them. Why don't you come with me and let's look at the video."

With the Detective sitting at the desk and the uniform leaning over his shoulder, they had a nice surprise. The camera and security unit were one of the modern ones. The large screen was split into four sections, showing the action on the four cameras. One was the outside that was above the front door, one was in the rear hallway on the exit and bathroom and storage area. One was high and had a good view of the entire store and one was over the counter and cash register.

Getting the one important camera up and then the memory replay didn't take long. This modern system was made for dummies. The two watched as they got the screen view to a few minutes before the incident. The store was suddenly full of hoodies, boys walking around and grabbing small items from different shelves.

Watching patiently, they were finally rewarded with the

right shot that they looked on with complete fascination. A kid pulled out a gun, held it sideways and the old man began to pull out bills from the store. Evidently, he wasn't fast enough. They saw the gun buck as a shot went into the wall display of cigarettes and then the old man, who had a hand hidden, raised an arm and fired his own gun. He held it in the correct manner and the kid went down immediately.

Another kid ran over and leaned down to pick up the weapon from the floor, he jumped up to try to shoot the shopkeeper who was now smart enough to be down below the counter. The kid leaned over, looked up and then ran from the store with the gun.

The Detective backed up and stopped the view at the first place where the gun had appeared and stopped it so that he could take a shot with his cell. He heard a rustle and realized that the uniform was copying him and fishing out his own phone to capture the picture. Next after moving the screen scene forward, they both took pictures of the face of the kid who had picked up the weapon.

Now Damian found as he ejected the memory, that it was a disc so he put it in an empty storage flat plastic box. He pulled down a new one and inserted it into the memory section of the computer and turned everything on for security.

"Give this to the Supervisor. But we both know who to look for that has a weapon or hid it somewhere. Warn your fellow officers."

"Thanks," the uniform stepped back. "I'm Blackstone." He held out his hand.

Taking it in a firm grim, Damian introduced with his full name. Now he could leave and go back to cruising the dark streets. This robbery and death scene was on someone else's shoulders. Just a normal night in the city. There would be several other identical problems happening across the streets for the overworked patrolmen and the EMT people.

What he had to do next was find out how long this last girl was missing. The first two had been missing for four days or five nights. First the date, then the capture, next the MS with all Dom and no Safe Word. In the play there was death and cleaning them up and painting them to make them look like the cheapest whores. Finally, there was the placement of the body, a ritual that was important. Look what I can do, was the statement when the bodies were found.

This was a dangerous and very smart individual. This serial killer will not stop until they were stopped. This killer was like Damian, a night person. Who was out on the city streets every night that no one would notice that looked intelligent? Hearing far off sirens he thought about all of the police that were out alone, both in vehicles and walking a beat. He would not discount the night cops. There were also the EMT workers. There were some that were assigned to the late shift. Could one of them slip away from their partners to preform unspeakable acts. Of course, any intelligent person could find long hours sitting in the truck some way to provide an excuse for a little personnel time.

Pulling around a street cleaner, he had a new group to add to his list. Due to cut backs in the city budget, these people also drove the big units alone. Cab drivers were rare as there were not safe passengers in this end of town, but he passed one and added another group to his list that was getting long. But the degree of intelligence he felt that surrounded the killer would let him omit some people.

If the perp was a cop, an EMT worker or cab driver, he also would be studying for a higher job. He would have lab books or a day time requirement for some schooling. But in this day and age of Online College, a lot of people sought their finals or Masters on a computer. In his structured mind he began to cross off some of the people on jobs that would not be helpful for a person working on a degree. He realized that in small ways he might be bigoted, because he eliminated the street cleaners first.

Passing by an all night club, he saw the bouncer at the door and crossed that type of person off his list also or he did not add them.

For the next few nights, he cruised the streets and answered calls. As was his habit, he usually started his shift by going into the first busy floor of the Detectives' Division to the cubby that was reserved for him. There he might take a few moments to check for messages, return some, check for past information on his computer and talk to the others around him.

It was quiet on the third shift with few in the office. Standing behind his chair he went through the pink phone messages and discarded all of them. Then he noticed the yellow slip stuck to his screen. He sighed as he saw Maybelle heading his way.

At. 6'4" Damian was taller than most men in this office. Maybelle was a tall attractive woman and since she found out he was presently single she had been sending out signals. She had been too obvious, brushing up against him. Sometimes, patting him on the butt as they passed in the hall and leaning over his shoulder too far as he sat in his chair.

When noticed, the guys around him loved to tease him. Most were jealous and now someone whistled as she walked through the aisle that were only slightly higher than a person's waist. At least the dividers were solid and could be leaned on or have heavy boxes set upon for short time. But these were short enough to allow those walking to see around the long room. This time Maybelle had on a dress with the top buttons open too low to show the lacy bra. The other shift Lieutenants would have called her up on her clothes, but the third shift boss was too busy to worry about the small rules.

"Damian dear," the woman approached and put a bright

red fingernail on his chest as she moved in close. With a different thought than what she wanted, he grabbed her finger and used it first to put space between them, then he looked at it closely.

"Where do you buy your polish?"

His question caught her by surprise. "Well, uh, Macy's. You get great deals there." She pulled her hand back and in a female way spread her full hand out looking at the back and seeing all five nails. "Oh, the LT needs to see you."

Without a word, he turned away from his nemesis and headed back towards the boss's office.

"Oh, no. Their in the conference room. OCU is with him."

It took him a second to stand still and then take a different aisle to go where she indicated. That second of hesitation was due to the fact that members of the Organized Crime Unit were with his boss.

Walking the streets late into the night, Damian always saw the underbelly of the city. He knew there were three categories of organized crime and all of them were ugly. At the top and in the news and movies were the old ones run by families and people who had to earn a place within the tribe. It was hard to understand by most upstanding citizens, but those people caused the least amount of harm, keeping the problems among their own groups. There were Hispanic gangs. Walking under the weak or missing street lights, he had learned a lot about the different street gangs. There were Puerto Ricans, Cubans and Mexicans and they could be told by their colors and their tats. They all pretty much stayed in their own neighborhoods.

The worse of the brunch were the teens. There were roaming groups of teens who either had no homes or parents that made the homes hopeless. They were the most dangerous because they had no rules, they robbed when they were hungry for food, beer or drugs. They would kill without a thought and sometimes by accident. The worse part was that they were everywhere and fought with each other, killing or maiming bystanders.

Thinking of all this mess, Damian didn't want to get into the conference room, but he liked the Lieutenant or person often called Chief, and would not embarrass him. With one quick knock he entered the conference room to meet a couple of detectives in very nice suits.

"Detective Walker," Lieutenant Dright was standing, leaning against the display board on one wall. "This is the man who has the most knowledge of the late night streets in our district. I can loan him out to you for a week. But no longer as he is in the middle of a big case for us." The LT's voice was firm, but he didn't raise the level. He didn't need to shout to make a point. It was one of the traits that Damian liked about his boss.

Still the fact that he was being re-assigned without being asked rankled him. He swallowed his pride with his anger and pulled out a chair to sit with his new short time partners.

"So, what's the gig?" He looked them both in the eyes to evaluate them as they answered.

The woman spoke first. They both looked in their early forties which was where Damian was and he was surprised that they accepted him so fast.

"It seems that the Valducci's have a war on their hands. They own a couple of whore houses, but someone else has moved in to set some right in the neighborhood. When some of Valducci's made guys went over to discourage the customers, they disappeared. No one has seen them." She turned her hands over empty.

"Floating in the river?" Walker asked as he sat back in the hard backed chair.

"Nope," now the guy joined in. "They disappeared.

Walker frowned at the two well dressed detectives. "Are

we in business to help the crime loads find their missing thugs now?"

"No, we need to find out who can set up a new bunch of ladies and not be afraid of the big boys."

He thought about the words and realized they were now talking his language. He remembered the dim foggy streets and knew some facts. The teens didn't have whores, they just used whoever they could get their hands on and sometimes passed them around or sometimes became controlling, The Latins were pimps and had small numbers of ladies who walked the streets early in the night. They were in specific spots and knew the cops locations better than headquarters. It was the big guys that like to stay inside and set up houses. Of all the groups and even with the drug movement of the Latins, the old organized guys still had most of the funds. The Italians were known for bringing in the phony money from their home country and help from the Chinese. The USA was a country with a big red target on it and it was beginning to rot from the inside like an over ripe fruit.

Walking into the small conference room that had been set up for the investigation into the Whore Invasion Disappearances, Walker looked around with a frown. He had left his jacket and hat out at his cubby desk, but this brightly lit room was not his place. He preferred to be on the dark streets. He looked at the one wall with the white board already marked up with the erasable pens.

CHAPTER FOUR

In red at the top of two division, one listed the name Valducci and the second was Unknown. Underneath in in some words in black and some in blue were ideas and names, on both sides. Behind him he heard the others come in and move around the table to pull out chairs and sit down. They preferred starting their shifts by studying the problems and talking, lots of talking. He picked up one of the folders that had the entire information that was set for each of them and then walked back out of the room. He was headed to the dark streets for the real answers.

Before he got out of the car that he parked deep in a low garage, he took a moment to read through the file. There had been two of the Valducci men who had disappeared. There was the usual arrest photo and attached police page of descriptions. One of the men was a short over weight guy who pretended to work on the docks. The other was a bruiser who probably was used for muscle when needed. It would take a surprise or weapons to take these two out. Better still it would take a lot of effort to make their large bodies disappear, even in this immense dirty city.

The folder had a report on all the morgues, hospitals and holding areas where the bodies of these two made fellows might show up. Nothing. This was unusual as dead bodies popped up everywhere. Floaters were found in the two rivers or along the docks. The garbage complained about bodies in dumpsters and on the barges going to dump sites. The calls to 911 and Police about bodies in alleys and on gutters were more common than the ones for normal aide.

So, did someone take these two large bodies out of the city? Now it was time for him to hit the streets. It was long after midnight and he was in his long coat and hat. What he chose to wear kept him dry and warm from the early morning fog. Also, among the strange collection of people who were out in the dark city in all types of unusual clothes from elegant late night diners to drunks and of course the bums who were hoping to scavenge. His hat and coat was different enough to fit and not shout cop.

The first stop on Walker's mental list was the whore shop right around the corner from where he had found the dead girl only a few nights ago. He knew a lot of the workers there and the one woman in charge. It was an independent shop and was fairly safe for the women with no kids involved.

The area where a lovely woman had laid out in ugliness. Taking one last look down the narrow side street, Walker walked through the open door of the business without a sign or name. If you didn't know what it was, you were not welcome. But word of mouth brought plenty of customers to this place.

Two scantily clad ladies immediately were up against him with the heavy smell of perfume and wide smiles.

"What will it be tall man? How about a five hour all the way?" The short one was pitching with her words and her hands on his ass.

"Or if you're in a hurry, I can be on my knees in seconds. I have napkins to cover your zipper to keep you neat and clean, handsome." This one was already working at the front of his pants.

From behind them a voice with the right words stopped them. "Cops don't pay."

They stepped back and disappeared behind the many thick dark red curtains. The voice was from Megan, the woman who was in charge of the place. "Of course, so far, Detective Walker has never taken advantage of our services."

"I have a couple of questions." He tipped his head back to allow her to see his face under the shadow of the brim of his hat.

"Okay," Megan turned and expected him to follow. "I have coffee or whiskey in my office."

Not one to resist either offer, he followed Megan to a place that he a visited a time or two before. For those who had not been invited past the thick drapes and down a dark hall, they would have been disappointed at the lady's office. It was well lit and as normal as any office in a small business could be seen anywhere. Plenty of metal file cabinets, a large wooden desk with a modern flat screen computer and a couple of comfortable chairs.

There were no windows, but on the low case where there was a coffee maker and all the makings with a built-in small fridge below were also the bottle of whiskey and glasses.

The coffee she handed him was strong and black and laced with top shelf whiskey. He always enjoyed visiting with this lady. "So, problems? "He nodded his head at the computer screen.

"No, it seems to have worked itself out. My girls are smart. What can I do for you, Detective Walker?" She met him eye to eye.

"Besides a dead girl around the corner and a couple of new places opening up downtown, now why would you think I would be in here?" Walker's dull grey eyes did have a sparkle now.

"Well," talking between sips of coffee, Megan treated the conversation serious. "The dead body was not one of our and the girls of mine who saw it said it really wasn't a paid pro."

"Yep, we got that information after checking her out. Someone either hated her or wanted us to have a different idea about her. What about the new places?"

"I haven't lost any girls in fact I have had to turn down some applications. It seems there is a lot of unrest in all solid houses."

Solid was a word for houses that were set up in permanent locations. They were located away from residential areas and were busted once in a while. But they would open again in another boarded-up building with the same girls and more customers. Megan was a dying breed, an honest owner with a hidden partner who only had this one location.

Finishing his coffee, he knew he had gotten all he could from this gracious lady. It was time to get back on the streets. He would walk and watch. He would listen and talk to a few regulars and probably even arrest someone. It was a night in the city and there was a scream far away, but too distant for his help.

Going home early, made him decide to hit the streets early the next night. He skipped going into the bright office and drove into his favorite area of the city. It was a busy night and surprised him since it was midweek. Even before he got out of his car he heard a call for a detective to answer for uniforms who had found a serious problems. The code also indicated dead body so he turned on the lights and floored the powerful engine. Within minutes he was at the location of the couple of lit up black and whites.

Leaving his coat and hat in the car let everyone see the gold shield on his belt. They could also see the unusual holster with the double extra magazines for the Magnum Research Desert Eagle 50 Action Express 6in Polished Chrome Pistol. His black belt held leather pockets on the sides that contained cuffs, a taser, and his cell and even some zip ties. Life had taught him to be prepared.

But he wasn't prepared for what was waiting at this particular call. They had found the missing Valducci thugs. He was pointed to the cop in charge who led him down the nice entrance to the above average downstairs apartment. The two large men, one short and fat and the other a big bruiser were poised at the dining room table.

Every officer from the ones on the beat all the way up to the guy with four stars on his collar had the mug photos of these two. There was a strong BOLO out on them but by this time, if they were found they would smell and be hard to recognize. Yet here they sat, in clean suits, looking like they had only been dead for a few hours.

"These are the made guys of the Valducci gang, right Detective?" The uniform looked back at other uniforms who were smart enough to not come into the room. Reaching in his pocket as he stood part way in the room, he pulled out the standard blue thin rubber gloves.

"How many of you guys have been in here and how many of you touched them?" Walker asked in his deep voice as he pulled on the hand covers but still did not move.

"Well," the cop next to him looked back again at his buddies. He was smart and wanted his friends to be on board with him. "Me, and Fred and Justin. We kept everyone else out and when we were sure what we had found we put in a call for a detective."

"Good. Now put in a call for a Supervisor and CSI." With those words Walker took a couple of steps forward to allow him to gently touch each man on the neck. He was able to be certain that the men were dead but had only been that way for about a day. But he was not going to state that fact. Stepping back, he pulled out his phone and called his Chief. He liked the man and would let him get here before the crowd.

There was one thing that really bothered him. These men had not been killed as soon as they had disappeared. Someone had been able to take charge of these guys who were used to fighting under any circumstances. A single gun in the face of the big guy would not take him prisoner. Even short and fat was known to clear out a bar room when someone made a mistake and said something he didn't like.

Standing and looking at the neat suits the guys were wearing, it was hard by the pale discolored look of death on their faces to see if they had taken a beating. They would have to be laid out in the morgue to get a real understanding of what had happened and how they had ended up here.

"How did you find them?"

The uniform beside him cleared his throat and pulled out a small pad. This guy had done everything by the book. "The lady that rents it, Mrs. Ruth Livinstein, came home to find them. Says she doesn't know them and called the police about invaders or robbers." He looked over his shoulder at his friends. "We have kept her outside letting her set in one of our cars. We are the only ones who have been inside even with all the arguments from our brothers who want to check out the scene."

Pulling out his phone and the pin that came with it, Walker made his notes right on the screen. He loved technology. Looking at the officer, he got the guys badge number and last name. "I'm making a note of your ID. It is a positive note because you have handled this in a very smart manner. Thanks. You will be checked out by CSI when they get here so you might as well stay close. The Supervisor will give instructions to everyone else when they get here."

Hearing the sirens outside, Walker recognized one of them as the higher tone of the EMT unit. "Hey, tell the guys outside to keep the Emergency guys out of here."

All three stepped out in the hallway, evidently relieved to have something to do. It wasn't long before the Lieutenant Barkin was standing in the doorway. "I'm not coming in, but it is obvious who is sitting at the table. This is a cruel joke. Until the supervisor gets here, it looks like I'm the boss so I'm going to take a position on the outside doorway."

"The young uniform who was in here is smart."

"Good to know." Barkin left, and not moving so as not to disturb footprints, Walker began to take pictures with his phone. With the doors all open to the outside, he could hear all the movement and ruckus up on the sidewalk and street. He knew the uniforms were pouring in and had their hands full keeping the gawkers back. He believed that the Lieutenant also had them checking out all the parked cars. You never know when you might get lucky.

"Looks like the night supervisor got caught up in a hit and run that involves one of the Council men's kids. So, I am it. I need you to go talk to the lady that has this place and then get her a room at a nice hotel on the Police tab." Barkin was not going to enter the crime scene room as he stood outside the doorway.

"Sure, boss." Walker felt he had spent enough time in the room and needed a breath of fresh night air. He pulled out his phone to make sure he had the lady's name correct as he approached the car where she was sitting. They had left the door open and someone had gotten her some coffee.

"Mrs. Livinstein, I'm Detective Walker. How are you doing?" Damian wanted to try a friendly approach first.

"Well, this has been a bit too much. I returned from my book club meeting to find what I thought was a robbery at first. I saw the men and ran back out and call 911 from the sidewalk. I can't believe that people were inside my home. How am I ever going to feel safe in there again?"

Looking at the lady, she seemed to be in her late fifties, but it was hard to tell in these days. Her hair was a light brown, almost a blond and caught up in back with one of those big plastic clips. She had some make up on but did not seem to overdo it and her ear rings were small gold and probably real.

"Was your door unlocked when you started to enter?" He

felt she was calm enough to answer some questions.

"No. That's what I've been thinking about. The nice policeman checked the back entrance and said it was still locked. How can crooks get in without breaking windows or doors?" Now her voice rose a little.

Making a note to ask the uniform about the back door and what other places the man had checked, he was concerned about this lady and crime lords. On the other hand, she was using old fashioned words like policeman and crooks.

Chapter Five

"And you're sure you never saw the men before?" Damian watched her carefully as she shook her head.

"Gracious no. They were ugly brutes and I got only a quick look and ran." Now she leaned back on the car seat.

"Mrs. Livinstein, we won't be able to let you stay in your home tonight. We can arrange for a room at one of the better hotels at no charge to you." He hesitated to see her reaction.

"Oh, no." She reached down and brought up a small cell phone. "I've called a friend and I'm going over there. I don't know if I can ever stay here."

Well, that solved a problem in an easy manner. He spent a couple of more minutes with her and then turned to a close uniform.

"Get her some transportation to where she wants to go. Report to your superior where she is staying so we can reach her. Get her cell number and details of where the location is." He made another note on his phone with the stylus and got a nod from the cop.

Glancing up, he now saw among the crowd of official vehicles was the CSI unit. A couple of them were talking to the right three uniforms, so he believed that situation was well in hand. They would check the guys out for any trace elements before releasing them for off duty. Now he returned down the steps to the open doorway to report to his boss.

"Hey LT. CSI is here."

Barkin was waiting by the inside doorway. "Great, they can give you and me some booties and better gloves. What do we need to check out first? Any ideas?" The LT always used his people and that made him a good leader.

"The lady has her own place to stay, so that is taken care of. She said the place was locked up, so we need to check every door and window and hole." Darian glanced at his phone but was satisfied.

Holding up for the two scientists who were dressed from head to toe in protective coverings, they both soon had some covers of their own. Simple face masks, good thin gloves and soft papers over their shoes.

Nodding at Barkin, the two separated and began their lock search on each outside wall. First of all, Walker was impressed with the security on the narrow-slanted windows that were below the sidewalks. The fancy but heavy bars were on the inside and could only be unhooked from someone standing in the room. The windows had double locks and double glass.

First before entering a room, both men repeated the same process. Without inside lights, they turned on their small bright police hand lights and rolled them across the floor to highlight indentations in the carpet. That told them areas to avoid so they didn't disturb footprints for CSI. Next Walker found all the windows that gave an interesting view upward were all secure and had not been tampered with in this first room.

This apartment was full of large rooms that was immaculate with no dust and beautiful furniture. The lady had done well for herself. But what was her connection with the dead bodies in the other room? Checking out this upper class apartment, he let his mind wander to the few nights ago when he found the body on the side street.

Reading the Pathologist's report that Jean had sent to him, left nothing but more questions about the murder and still did not address the killer. The fact that the girl had been strongly restrained in a manner that left very few marks or bruises suggest some type of padded BDSM harness or straps. Most of those were strong but padded with something to protect the skin.

The girl had been mistreated in a harsh manner, her body used in every sexual manner, but then she had been bathed and dressed and polished and made up. When did a rapist take that much time and have that much expertise? Was this a complicated person who had a multi personality? That would make the final identity even more difficult.

The girl had been kept in captivity for a long while, as even an excited killer had to wait between erections to penetrate her again. Jean had stated that although the girl had been raped repeatedly in every orifice, no foreign objects had been used. So, it was personal for the killer, and so was the way the woman was dressed and cleaned and presented. There was a message in all of it that Damian felt he was on the verge of getting, but still did not understand.

They finished their rounds, after checking the ceilings of every closet. The boss sent Walker out to talk to the street people, believing he would get a better read on what was said or left out. By that time a second CSI team was inside and a morgue truck had arrived. Damian decided to move his car before the HQ truck showed up and he got blocked.

Once in the car, he sat in the dark two blocks away and took a moment to go through the photos on his cell phone. Using his fingers, he enlarged the face of the heavyset thug and finally did see some strange marks around the ears. It looked like burn marks on the edges, but he grunted as he realized it was the opposite. They were marks from being frozen.

Anger was burning from his toes up. It was an old anger that came from a different time and a period of hard training. It was a time in his life that was redacted in all the documents of his military records. But there were some things you could erase and some you could black out. But there were some things that would make their way to the surface when danger pushed too hard. Damian was beginning to feel the push.

Reading the different folders on the men that had been given to him, they were full of arrests and quick releases. There were pages of fancy footwork by expensive lawyers that brought forward proof of arrest errors, lost evidence, witness disappearances and plain mistakes.

He threw the folders down on the passenger seat when a notice came through for a call of shots fired and all officers to report. The address and cross streets were put out on the radio in the middle of his dashboard and Darian sat up, looking around. He was sitting only a half block from the location, but had heard nothing.

Dropping his hat over the folders, he got out and checked his weapon as he jogged quietly back in the direction of the address from the cop alert. Darian knew this area so well since he walked it so often so he realized that the problem was coming from one of the sex shops. As he reached the building in the dark, he plastered himself against the wall by the open door. Off in the distance he heard the wail of the sirens, but it would be a time before the black and whites were here. He decided to go in and see the situation.

Pulling up his weapon in both hands, he let it lead the way. Detective Damian Walker caught a gleam off the chrome of his pistol. He didn't carry the normal police issued Glock. Instead, he had long ago received the heavy weapon in his hands now for a deadly use. It was a Magnum Research Desert Eagle 50 Action Express 6in Polished Chrome Pistol. It could punch a hole through most metal and all the way through bodies. But it took a strong steady hand and a special eye to make a mark with this impressive gun. It was a show piece that he didn't bring out to flaunt in the office.

Inside and through the over decorated reception area, Damian stepped into the back hall where he heard a woman pleading.

"Please, I'm telling you the truth. We don't have a safe here."

"Bullshit. Everyone has a place where they store the fuckin' cash." The man's voice was rough but sounded older than Damian expected. Usually, the crime in this area was done by kids from the streets.

"I think the woman is telling the truth." Damian stepped into the doorway and had the gun on the one man in the room with what he assumed was the Madame. On the floor was a girl who was either unconscious or dead. Blood was around the downed girl's face where it was turned into the flooring.

"Dave, you got everything under fuckin' control." The voice was younger and came through the wall.

Deciding he had to do something quick before he got caught between to criminals, Damian jerked his gun as he stepped into the room. "Step away from the woman."

What the jerk did instead was with the one arm he was holding, he pulled her over and in front of him. He then put the small .38 pistol to her head.

"How about you back out of here or I blow her fuckin' head off?" There was desperation in the man's voice.

Looking at the man, Damian decided he was working with complete fools. The big man was fat and tall probably weighed in at 230 or 250 while the woman was small and thin. She was a tiny thing that hardly came to his chin. Damian had a lot of choices of where to shoot the asshole, but chose the one to close the deal. He barely moved the barrel and fired one shot. In his strong steady hands, the big gun was ready. The woman went down with the man, but immediately began to crawl away from his body. The man jerked a couple of times as his life ran out through the big hole in his forehead.

"Dave?" It was the voice of the other perp right behind the thin plaster wall.

Looking over at the woman, Damian motioned. "Stay down." He hissed and then turned and took one step to the wall. He fired four shots, each one at waist level about four inches apart in a row through the thin wall. He heard the scream of a man and began to move out of the room, his weapon in front.

Around a corner and through another door he soon found the other burglar on the floor, bleeding from two gut shots. The kid had dropped his small gun and was holding his gut with his knees drawn up.

Looking up at the tall man holding the chrome weapon on him, he had tears in his eyes but he could still talk. "I want a lawyer and to go to a hospital." He coughed a bit but no blood.

Stepping closer with the barrel directly on him, Damian looked at the four holes in the wall and down at the bleeding kid. They learned so fast on the streets. Shaking his head, Damian decided no one would check the magazine in his big chrome gun. Without any emotion he shifted the barred and pulled the trigger. Another hole appeared in the crumpled kid, one right in his heart and there was no more movement or sounds.

Checking the end of the hall for any more thieves, he returned to the lady on her knees and helped her move out to the reception area. By that time the lights of the black and whites were filling the window.

Chapter Six

Detective Damian Walker had gone through the shooting inspection routine before. It gave him time in the office at night to catch up on reports. Like everyone else who is a cop, he hated the people that worked in the Internal Affairs Department. Still, he understood the need, as there had been some legitimate cops who had been on the take or helped the wrong people.

But in their enthusiasm to fill their reports, the IAD took up a lot of peoples' time looking into issues that should be rubber stamped with one quick glance. Perhaps they were bored.

Coming in for his shift, that was the late one with few people in the long office room with its division of cubbies. They had a new Chief and he asked even detectives to join the quick announcement meeting at the start of each shift. Damian waited to be one of the last to enter and leaned against the back wall. This way he could leave early.

The new Chief was a surprise when he showed up some time ago as he looked like he should be on retirement. A heavy hair of almost white grey color and a stiff mustache to match, he had wrinkles around his eyes that made him look like he was always angry. Damian was astonished when he found he like the man after the few times they talked. The man went right to the point and didn't waste time.

Chief Reede ran his meetings the same way, to the point and short. To his shock, as he turned to slip back out the door since the only thing of importance was a mention of the

Valducci gang, the Chief called his name. This meant Damian kept the wall upright as everyone else left.

Not having to move as the Chief approached, Damian waited for whatever was on the old man's mind.

"I put some pressure on IAD and you are back on duty. Now I know you have a burr up your ass about the Valduccis, so this is your chance to go out and get something to hang on the whole fucking group." The Chief tapped him once on the chest and left.

When he got to where his jacket was holding up a chair, there was a large internal envelope on his desk. Ripping it open he put the big pistol into the special leather holder and his body felt better with the weight. The case with his ID and badge he slipped into a back pocket. Grabbing a small police issue tablet that would tie into details when he needed them, he left with the jacket in the other hand.

There was one thing he had discovered, he did better work setting in the deep leather seats of the a low slung dark Charger with tinted windows than he did under the over bright office lights.

There was no need for folders as all the information on the V gang was at his fingertips on this one small tablet. Thank the Gods for Apple and programmers. This was getting him nowhere. There had to be a guy who finally ended up with the money and passed the orders down. It might be someone with the Valducci name or some other old world title. But to stop this gang he had to ignore the street hoods and get to the next level.

The first job was to follow the money. Damian sat down the street from a sex shop that was listed on his pad as owned and operated by the V gang. It was next door to a pawn shop that did not do much business. That made the pawn shop as a front for laundering bills. Even if the Treasury Department got involved, it was tough to tie anything to such a business.

It took him three nights of following deliveries and hand offs before he was sitting in front of a mansion with a neat lawn and a lit long driveway. The help had left for the day at around seven as the man liked his privacy. There were two hired security guards, so that meant no alarms.

The dark Charger was parked up against the wall that tied into the property from another who was more careful. The dark car was invisible within the bushes even from the rare headlights that passed. Popping the trunk, there were now three levels inside the roomy area. The first was what people expected with the small tire. But that would slide up and reveal that a second exposed nothing but weapons and ammo of all types and some that were illegal.

The bottom level had what Damian called his work tools. He was already dressed in black tight fitting comfortable clothes. There were removable coverings over his shoes and he set aside a set of latex gloves. He pulled on a standard dark face mask that had become popular after Covid19. He grabbed a flat backpack that was already packed. The comfortable weight of his favorite friend, he pulled out and kept in one hand, looping the pack over a shoulder.

Moving silently across the manicured lawn, making sure he stayed in shadows, his first target was taking a cigarette break. White smoke marked the position and the head was in a perfect position when it was hit by the blackjack. There was hardly any noise as the big man holding a long gun folded and went down.

It took Damian ten minutes to use duct take to have the man on his stomach, mouth sealed and arms together. The heels were strapped together than bent to bind them to the wrists in back. To ease the man, Damian pushed him over on his side even though the guy was still unconscious. He took everything from the guy's pockets and put them in his backpack.

Now it was on to the next security stiff. The next guy didn't make it as easy as Damian approached the guy turned at the last second. There was a tussle while Damian prevented the man from bringing up or firing his weapon. The man was strong but used his body in the wrong way. His intent was to overpower with no skills in fighting. It took Damian two punches, one to the lower gut and the other with a flat hand to the throat to shut the aggressor down.

As the man choked, Damian tied him up with the duck tape in the same manner as the previous guy. He was also turned on his side as he blinked back angry tears. Now Damian moved on into the mansion and through to the wide game room where a hefty middle aged gentleman sat watching something on a giant TV.

AS Damian stepped around the big low long curved couch where the man was sitting, the man turned.

"What the fuck?" Those were the only words the man got out as Damian hit him on the side of the neck with the blackjack baton. The man jerked sideways and then didn't move.

When Geo Valducci woke up it took him a few seconds to fight through the pain in his head and understand where he was located. He could hardly move his head due to something wrapped around his neck and holding his head in place. Blinking several times, Geo realized he was out on the lanai and that he was naked, sitting in one of the large metal chairs.

Trying an effort, Geo realized he couldn't move. His was taped to the chair with both arms and legs strapped in tightly and even his body held in place. He took a deep breath and felt the tape around his chest holding him to the expensive seat that he had been so proud of when showing off to guests.

"Help." Geo went ahead and yelled out to the security guards. But a quiet voice drew his attention to a man who was down on a heel across the lanai near the house wall.

"No one can hear you. They are all tied up right now."

Geo frowned at the dark figure in the shadow. "You know you are fuckin' dead already." He snarled at the man. This bastard didn't realize who he was robbing.

"Geovanni Arturo Valducci. I have a question. Who do you send the money on up to?" The man's voice was low and steady.

Geo was confused. Surely this man had come to rob the house so why was he asking about the payments? "Fuck you. When my boys hear about this they won't stop hunting you."

"This new hose is an interesting gadget. I've seen it advertised on TV. It grows when water is turned on and shrinks when the nozzle is open and water off, right?"

"Who the fuckin' cares. Untie me and I will let you walk away." Geo was slobbering as he spoke.

"You should care." Then the man turned on the valve at the wall. The hose fattened up and Geo realized what was holding his head up. The hose was wrapped around his neck several times and as it filled with water it shut off his ability to breath or talk. Geo realized he was being strangled by the hose unless the man turned off the water and opened the nozzle. He wiggled his hands and lifted his feet and then the man did turn off the spigot and opened the nozzle.

The hose shrank and suddenly Geo's head could move and he grabbed a deep breath.

"Now, who do you pass the bulk of the money onto?"

Chocking on his words, Geo finally rasped. "Even if I tell you, they will kill us both."

The man moved his hands in the shadow and then turned on the wall spigot. The hose began to tighten and Geo was being killed by the god damned special hose. He tried to move his head or tilt it but there was no room and he heard cracks that he thought might be bones or something in his neck. He was wiggling everything, ready to tell this bastard anything. Let the guys on top tell and skin this asshole.

At last, the pressure on his neck went away as the water drained out of the expanding hose and it shrank in size. It took Geo only a few seconds to spill out the name and even the address of his uncle who ran the show and gave the deep orders. Let Uncle Dimi handle this dead man walking.

Those were some of Geo's last thoughts as the water spigot was turned back on but the nozzle was not touch. The man in black only walked away as the advertised hose did its job.

Chapter Seven

In the quick meeting the next night, Chief Reede announced the death of a mob head in the Valducci gang. Again, he called Damian's name out as everyone was ready to leave and the two walked together back toward the office area.

"Detective, this happened last night. I know it was across town from your usual beat, but go on over there. The CDI unit is still there as it was only reported today and it is what I want you on with the Valducci gang." Reede nodded once and turned away. That meant that Detective Walker had his orders.

That was fine with Damian as he grabbed his jacket, waved at the only other guys still in their section and headed out. It didn't take him long to pull up to the yellow tape around the mansion and get out of the low car. He attached his shield to the leather jacket he had put on and let the street cop hold the tape up for him.

Up by the front steps was the large truck for the inspection group and another dark standard detective car. Damian walked in slowly, looking the place over with all the lights on and extra spot set up in several rooms. One was high lighting a large vault that must have been hidden behind a large mirror that was now pulled out on hinges into the room.

Watching the busy people for only a moment, he approached the one person who was standing still with her hands on her hips. This had to be the Supervisor assigned to the entire crime scene for CDI.

"I'm Detective Walker, head of the Valducci project from

Station Twelve." Damian didn't bother to hold out a hand. They were not here to socialize but to observe.

"CSI is gone. A whole group of frustrated techies that couldn't find a single hair or fiber out of place." The Supervisor frowned as she was looking at the additional photos taken of the spigot. The hose was gone, probably safe in a sealed carton in the CSI truck.

All of the tape around the chair had been carefully removed and was also moving in that same truck in separate bags. But the chair was marked and the area around it had all kinds of chalk marks on the cement. There was also lots of black dust from the fingerprint people.

"The security guy said it was one guy. One man who overpowered healthy trained guards and tied them up then took the gang boss down and brought him out here naked," she tipped her large pad to show a photo on the screen. "Then this batman strangled the boss with a fancy hose and left, not stealing anything."

"Well, the CSI people are good. I will check with them tomorrow night." Damian held out his own tablet and let the reports pop up.

"Yeah, even Batman made some mistakes. They can tie the ends together of all that duck tape to the roll that he has somewhere. The guard he over powered said he was wearing a regular black Covid face mask. They were sold and there are records. It is the work of the computer guys."

"Yep," Damian nodded. "In this day and age it would take a really smart guy to outfox the techies." He waved a thanks to the Supervisor and slowly left the scene. He remembered the smell of the burning of the short pieces of duck tape. Then there were the many stops to drop small garbage sacks into gas station containers and at the Dairy Queen Drive Thru when he went inside. There were some things in the big dumpsters, but they were also small items in dirty bags he picked up inside and added his items.

He had changed from latex gloves to tight black leather ones on the way back to his apartment. By the time he was home, everything he had worn down to his socks were disposed and he had on clean clothes and shoes of a Detective. He even put on the hat at the right angle as he got out of the car to go up to his unit and take a long hot shower.

That had been before, but this night he was moving his car back onto the street and heading it into town. He needed to do some checking on a special neighborhood and a new hideout for an important top crook. Around two am when the fog came in, he parked the car and putting on his long jacket and hat, he walked slowly from block to block. He was just one more single figure out on the street, looking for a buy.

Then he saw what he was looking for, a broken down garage that was seeing too much business. A pawnshop with dark windows even though it had an old sigh on the door that said open. To top the picture off was a couple of guys, not together, but leaning against the damaged brick walls and watching the traffic.

The cars that went in or out were either top of the line Caddies or tricked out low riders. There was a food delivery, not pizza and beer but a load from one of the high priced Jewish delis. That meant in Damian's mind someone was living in the upstairs apartments but had to come and go through the garage. This whole two story building was not approved for occupation.

The next night as the Chief was ending the short brief, Damian was not the first one out. He waited and walked with Reede back to the Chief's office. Standing in the doorway, he waited for the man to ask the question.

"What you got for me, Walker?"

"I have the location of where I think the next level up is located in the Valducci Gang." Damian had his pad ready and turned the flat small screen with the photo of the street on it and laid the tablet on the boss's desk.

"Well, it has all the earmarks of the standard hole. Where did you get this information and is it clean?" The Chief was checking on how sure the information was and where it came from.

"I have a CI who I trust. The guy is in serious trouble and I help him out now and then." Every Detective and even some street cops had confidential informants that they depended on for tips on things or people that might help the CI get a buck or out of jail.

The old man slid the tablet back. "What do you need?"

"Some listening devices and phone taps on the garage and pawnshop."

"Done, now go do your job." Damian like a boss who made fast decisions and didn't waste time talking. By the time he got to the basement to draw from the equipment department, the paper was pouring out of the fax machine. Since there was only one man who worked this area on the late shift and did the job due to permanent injury, Damian offered to go and get what he needed.

That meant he could also pick up a few other items he needed, like new rolls of duck tape, standard black Covid masks, and a few extra listening devices. Everything except two small boxes of listening devices went into his pockets.

The cop on the desk was grateful he did not have to go down the long shelves to hunt for a couple of boxes. Most of the cops, especially the detectives would wait at the window or sit in a chair while they expected him to walk on his sore legs to fill their orders. They had no idea how big this storage area was and how many rows took up the dim aisles he had to travel to fill their damn orders.

He was grateful when this tall officer with the hard grey eyes always offered to get his own order. The detective never took very long and always showed him what was retrieved as the two boxes were held out in one hand. Not that anyone had done an inventory since he had been put on this job in three years. Who knew what stuff filled the shelves and gathered dust back behind him?

They both signed the proper place on the paper and he scanned the boxes so that he could input the info into the computer. Sometime a new supply would come in with other things on the day shift. Not his problem. But he was too young and the pay for injury discharge was too low, so this was still his regular income as if he were still on the street. He could handle the quiet night shift, especially with a polite detective who didn't act like a jerk.

Once Damian got his supplies, he needed someone who had an in to the garage and even upstairs. For the rest of the night he hid in the dark cover of a door down the street and watched the cars come and go. There were also street people, some dealers and some hookers. Now he had a choice of who to enlist.

Street dealer and cheap hookers could both be turned to used as either informants or doers. But on the second night of watching, he noticed a girl that he knew. He had busted her on the street when she had tried to steal from a drunk who was passed out. She had a record of many busts from being in cheap houses or on the streets. She didn't have a pimp.

Now he needed to track her down and draft her for a quick project. This meant he spent his next few nights in his car with the passenger window down, driving slow and asking pros where he could find Josie Clamp. He had her dossier pulled up on his tablet that included several photos taken over the last couple of years. In each of them the life had taken its toll. The beautiful young girl had yellow skin and was now too thin. Drugs and malnutrition and the rough life had aged Josie. He wondered when she had actually slept a full eight hours?

At last, a disgusted whore who was leaning down in his window at an angle that allowed him to see her full breasts, nipples and all, frowned.

"I give head much better than that thin slut." She pulled back and then nodded at someone on the corner. It was Josie who was smoking a cigarette and waiting to catch cars as they slowed to turn. With very little traffic this late, a lot of the ladies were leaving so Damian pulled up and stopped.

"Hey handsome. I've got what you want." Josie also leaned over to allow a look down her low blouse.

"Get in." His voice was low and he had the button on unlock for her door. She didn't hesitate. Waiting this long she was grateful to get off her feet. She was also used to taking orders.

The strong odor of smoke, heavy cologne and body sweat blew over from her as he left the window open.

"So, what cha' want, handsome? I can do it all." She was digging in a pocket and pulling out a crushed package of cigarettes.

"No smoking." His voice rasped as he turned down a dark closed alley. He knew the place and no one would bother them here.

"Sure, babe. You're the boss." She kept her hand in the pocket holding onto the crushed box.

Pulling to a stop in the dark, he left the car running but shut off the lights. He pulled the lever on the steering wheel that adjusted the wheel upward. Then he reached down and slid the seat all the way back and twisted to face the worn out girl.

"Okay honey, some cash up front and I can straddle you or lean over." She was adjusting herself on her own seat.

At that point Damian pulled his long jacket back and exposed the gold shield attached to his belt.

"Hey, no problem. I serve a lot of cops, honey. I give service men discounts." She looked at his face and when there was no emotion, she cleared her throat. "Or hell, a freebee is okay, I guess."

"Hold up, Josie, I need a favor."

The girl was already leaning towards him, her hands reaching for his pants' zipper. "Sure baby, any way you want it." She waited a minute to hear what type of sex was on this John's mind. She had done it all and had all of it done to her, some of it painful.

So now it was time to get down to business for both of them. She needed the cash and maybe a favor from a cop and he needed to put her into a dangerous situation. Ain't life grand.

It started with his threat of arresting her and getting her in jail long enough to be clean. That brought the tears. She begged and promised him the greatest suck off he had ever felt as she described how she would suck him so deep he would think she was bottomless. What they ended up with was an agreement that suited both.

Josie agreed to take the listening devices into the garage and even try to get one upstairs. But . . .

CHAPTER EIGHT

Josie felt she had to have something on him, so she made him agree to let her go down on him. And she was right, the girl could open her throat to take his big cock so deep he was worried. But all thoughts went away with the pleasures of that tongue stroking the thick vein on the back of his stiff penis that ignored his brain.

This woman was worth more than a working girl on the streets. With one hand around the bottom of his member and her throat open to take more of him then most females couldn't handle, she took her other hand and gathered his balls. It was at that moment that she got Mount Vesuvius to erupt.

Grabbing a towel from the back seat he handed his big white handkerchief over to her. It didn't take long to clean up and get his pants up from his ankles.

After the session and when they both were upright, Damian drove them out and through an all night drive through for sandwiches and soft drinks. He had to wonder if this was the first solid food Josie had eaten in quite a while.

In the parking lot, as they ate, he opened the small boxes and set the recorders. He showed her how to take off the tape so they could be stuck anywhere. When they were done it was almost morning so he dropped her off and told her he would see her at midnight. He gave her a hundred and watched her slip up into the dirty stairs.

A good days' sleep, hot shower and a chicken biscuit with strong large coffee was a perfect way to start the midnight shift. Damian avoided the office and drove through the streets listening to the police radio. He swung by what he considered his important places, the streets where crime was prevalent and the sex shop doors were open.

Finally, controlling his patience, he picked up Josie at the ratty apartment building. He again gave her instructions on the two small devices and dropped her off two blocks over from the garage. Now all he could do was wait with two separate small recorders running. He had done the watching and waiting for years and learned the routine. He came prepared with a cool box in the back seat and already located an alley for a quick piss.

Josie was feeling better than she had in months. Even though the cop was asking her to do something that might get her in deep shit, she felt she could handle anything. The handsome tall detective with the grey eyes had got her a meal and given her a hundred dollar bill. It had been a while since she had serviced a john who paid that type of money. Things had been rough on the streets and since she had been on the sauce she didn't act as good or maybe take good care of her looks.

But with the bill he gave her she had gotten some real good stuff and was walking tall. She had a shower that was only lukewarm in the cheap hotel and had taken the time to brush her hair. She even put on clean clothes.

Feeling smart and the promise of another hundred dollar bill from the cop when she reported his assignment done, she didn't even try to attract the cars going by until she recognized one. It was a low rider all tricked out and she knew it was heading for the garage. She actually waved it down and the side window opened to show a face that she wasn't sure she knew. But mostly she didn't see the faces of the men she serviced.

"Hey, Josie. Lookin' to take on two?" The man leered at her with a crooked smile.

Deciding it was okay, she leaned down on the door frame and gave him a real smile. "I'd like to get out of the cold. You heading to the garage?"

The guys knew the different leaders and the top boss let whores stay inside at the garage for some free humping. It passed the time and let everyone stay under the eyes of the top boss.

Josie had to sit on the guy with the bad smile's lap while he hung onto her breast. The trip was short as they weren't far from the dark street with the garage. She didn't complain about the deep feel between her legs as she got out, but the men had to report to the back and she was left alone to straighten her skirt.

There was one other girl sitting on a bunk against a side wall and was hard to see over the many running and torn apart vehicles. Josie had been in here several times and was used to the layout. About half way back through the cars, tool cards and hanging cables, the garage turned into what some would call a bunk area and office space. There was one man with his back turned to everyone sleeping on a far bunk under a set of stairs. There were two sets of stairs going up, and were used by anyone. But there was always a man up above on the top crossing or balcony between the steps. He had one of those big powerful automatic weapons.

Not looking up at the guard above, Josie assumed that the men took turns on that duty overlooking the garage. So, the front half of the garage was a high open area mostly hidden under the hanging lights, and the back was built into two levels. The bottom was open and used for the men who came and went. The upper was supposed to have an office for the so called big boss and even a fancy apartment.

To help the cop and get another one of those big bills, she needed to plant one of these tiny thingies near the phones, downstairs and if possible, to plant one upstairs. For the first time in as many days and nights, Josie was able to walk upright and comfortable in her clunky heels. She was nervous for a number of reasons.

This was the first time she was in the garage when she was not deliberately brought in by one of the men. She was also trying to do something that will get her a hole in her head from one of the many guns that were inside this building. Josie was feeling good as she had some royal stuff in her body from the extra bill the detective had given her.

Taking her time and imagining herself as a real spy from a movie with Angelina Jolie, she took her time. She made her way between aisles and finally smiled as she got to the long table with the phones. For some reason no one was occupying any if the chairs, so she pealed the small tape of the tiny gadget and leaned into the long solid table trying to decide where to put it.

Suddenly she was grabbed by the hips.

"Perfect, lean over more, Josie." It was the guy from the car and he was pushing up her short skirt. He was even kicking his feet between hers and she knew what was coming next. Sex was nothing to Josie, except if she could make some money from it. The only time she remembered it was when it hurt. But the guys in this garage were only interested in quickies or a suck.

She didn't care that someone yelled to the guy behind her as he shoved into her dry and pushed again and again. With her mind on something else, she held on firmly with one hand and slid the other under the table. Right below the wires to all the connection from outside for phones she stuck the what-d'you-call-it and got a different satisfaction this time from the fast fuck.

Three or four jerks and the asshole was done, leaving her with oily slop on her thighs. Now she needed a rag or towel. Looking around as the short termed guy was getting high fives from friend, Josie knew that was a large dirty restroom in the back and another upstairs.

With her skirt back down and still firm on her heels, she walked directly to the closest stairs. It was a rough built wooden set hanging loose with thick rails on both sides for the first part. This was not the first time she had allow cum to dry on her body, but now she had an excuse to go up these rough heavy steps.

There were many doors open except the heavy one at the end near the other stairs. She had never been close to that and felt it led back into a hallway to the back apartments. Josie had heard the men talking about the fact that there were only two apartments up above and only one was occupied. She and the other girls were smart enough to not ask about who might be in that one apartment.

One of the open doors let her see a lot of small computers and the type of phones that could be carried around without wires or cords. Still there was a ton of wire and cord running under the desks pushed together and in bundles to the side walls. There was a guy with his back to her and on the phone with his feet up on the corner of one of the desks. Without hesitation Josie walked in. The first thing she did was walk over to a shelf that had a large pile of some type of rags. With one in hand, she made a large noise with her shoes on the floor as she acted like she stumbled against the side of the desk.

"What the fuck?" The guy on the phone jumped up, turned to looked in all directions. He wasn't the smartest rower in the boat as he looked out the door first and then saw the woman in the room with him. He almost dropped his gun, trying to get it out of the back of his belt and finally was on his feet in an awkward stance.

"What are you doing in here bitch?"

"I was looking for the bathroom." Josie waved the rag and

pulled up her skirt to show him her shaved pussy and she began to wipe her upper legs. "This will do and then I can go back down stairs."

Leaning to clean herself she had one hand on the end of the desk.

"Damn right. I should cap you for being in here. Get the fuck out." The man waved the gun all around.

"Got cha" She smiled and let her hand slip. She fell forward with the dirty smudged rag making a streak on the desk and pushing some wires aside. Hidden under the rag as she lay across the desk, she pulled the tab off the thingummy and there was a phone base that she had knock over. She stuck the tiny item to it as she turned it over and straighten up the rest of the items.

"Sorry." She continued to adjust things and swipe the dirty rag over things.

"Stop that, bitch. Get out of here before I shove you over the railing." Now he was getting nervous.

Standing up and pulling her skirt down, she held up her hands and began to back up to the door. As soon as she could, she waved good-bye at him and tottered out onto the balcony. Now it was time to get out of here.

For Damion, leaning against a dark doorway, the waiting and watching had been longer than normal for him. He was always used to spending time in the dark and watching for clues and people to make the wrong step. But to wait for the woman that he had used to come out of that garage, had been the longest hours on his nerves that he had endured.

Before the sky changed, Josie came out arm in arm with another woman. They stopped the first car that slowed down when the driver saw them. Damian figured they had a way to pay for a ride.

Damian walked the few blocks through the alleys to where he had parked his car and got in to rest. He put his hat on the passenger seat and reached behind to pull a dark blanket off the pile of mechanical boxes that looked like a display from Radio Shack. One stack were automatic recorders. Each machine would start recording when voices were talking on phones. These units would record 24/7 and he would pull the tapes to listen for prime words. This meant for the next few nights he did the boring detective work they never tell on the TV shows. Hours and hours of listening to idiots trying to sound like wise guys and making stupid plans to steal from honest people. Sometimes he sat in the quiet bright office cubby with fat ear covers over his head and checking on the alerts.

When a tape stopped on the word 'Mister' he would play the section to listen to the conversation, hoping to get real info on the gang or the hidden man up in the apartment. He would listen to certain tracks in the car without the headsets, letting the voices from the phone bounce off the inside. Damian even listened in his small apartment, letting them put his to sleep and wake him up.

The opportunity came not when he got a big tip on the hidden man up in the apartment, but a different more interesting bit of information. Replaying the call from the start, Damian had a clear picture of the inside of the dirty garage.

The big man called Supo came down the stairs and motioned to a couple of the other thugs to come over as he went to the table with all the phones.

"I need to make a couple of calls so I want cha' all to listen. Saves me time of repeatin." The man pulled out a chair and picked up a middle phone and dialed a phone.

"Hey Choko, its me. Yeah."

"I didn't get a name on my phone Supo. What gives?" The man Choko was speaking on a cell.

"I'm using the garage's special phone. The boss needs you over here on Wed. We are all going out to raid that new pussy shop that opened right next to ours. It is to be a full slaughter to teach them a lesson. Bring Mark." Supo's voice sounded tough but there was some humor underneath.

"On it. Lookin for some good action. Who all is goin?"

Choko nodded at the guys in the garage. "Everyone. We will take the whole team and do this right. Ya clear?"

"Clear and ready. I will get some special ammo and make sure Mark is sober." With that the call was over.

"So you guys heard the order. What do you have to do to get ready?" They all looked around and then started moving in different directions. First some of them needed to load up on a hit from their favorite that they had to keep secreted away from each other.

A couple were also smart enough to head to the back where there was a locker full of weapons and ammo and police vests. There they had their choice of all the weapons that were illegal on any list from state all the way up to federal. These guys chose the full autos and extra clips then went out to get their good feelings.

Chapter Nine

Supo was busy chasing out the couple of girls that were still staying around. This was not the time to have loose ears. What Supo did next was pick one of the guys that he felt he could trust and send him out to gas up Sobo's large Cadillac SUV and get an extra can of gas.

Supo had never felt so good. He was giving orders and everyone was jumping at his voice. Maybe his time had come. He would prove to the guy upstairs that they would burn the whore house down with not only the sluts but some of the Bluetag gang along with the whole smear.

He would get enough together so that they could converge on the address both the front and the back. They could trap everyone inside with a lot of fast gun shots and then some gas at the front door and the back and boom. Yep, he had it all laid out and ordered in pizza for everyone.

There was someone else buying gas in cans. It was Damian who was filling up four of the 5 gallon cans. This time he had drawn out a standard cop sedan and the big trunk held his load with no problems. He listened to the police radio and checked the garage area and went home at daylight to get a good rest.

The next night, after a good meal at a Denny's that served late and breakfast type meals all the time, he walked out to the sedan. This time he was dressed a little different, so in the car in the parking lot he took some time to finish his special look. He was in a special black military outfit with pockets, but the type that moved easily and didn't make a sound. He put on the military vest that was stronger than the police issue. His pants were tucked into the high soft boots that were laced up and he put on leather gloves that were so soft they felt like a lady's ass. He could pick up something thinner than a dime while wearing these gloves.

The shirt he wore had a hoodie that he pulled up over his head and low over his eyes. In one of his many pockets with a lot of interesting items, he had the standard Covid black face mask. Taking his time to drive to the garage, Damian wanted to allow the Valducci gang time to get out on their jerk for the night.

Watching the overhead doors and the small one, after another hour there was no activity. The crew was gone so Damian pulled the sedan up close to the side door and popped the trunk. He carried two of the cans with him when he entered the door in a noisy manner.

When he stepped back outside, he made a quick call to Chief Reede's private number. "My CI tells me the entire Valducci gang is going to pull a raid at 12245 Monrose." He hung up before the Chief could ask questions and carried the other two cans inside. He would trust on that older man to act on the tip.

"Hey, stupid, Hands up."

The shout came from a man up on the balcony.

"I brought Supo's gas cans. They are full." Damian walked through the disabled vehicles, staying in the dark to not let the guy see him.

"You fuckin asshole. They already left. Get the hell out of here."

Damian had a forty-five with a suppressor on it to keep the noise down. It was a gun that could not be traced back to anyone but the silencer cut down on the accuracy. He needed to get close. This time the brainless guard helped him by coming down the stairs to the bottom step. The long gun the idiot held was pointed at the floor.

The first shot from the forty-five was in the guard's forehead and the guy slid backwards against the wall before sitting down. As the black figure passed him, there was another puff from the silencer as a matching hole appeared in his head.

From the recordings and watching, Damian knew about another guard within the apartment. Going up the stairs, he was careful to step to the outside of each wood plank where they would not make a sound, still fastened solid. Going down the back hallway to the heavy doors, he knew that only one apartment was occupied.

The gang member inside the ante room when Damian opened the door was totally unaware that he was a dead man walking. He began to raise his long gun as he realized he was looking at a black ghost when there was a soft puff sound and then two more.

The man stumbled backwards, still trying to bring his auto up. What he did do was hit the trigger and a dance of bullets peppered the floor as the dead man also fell.

Stepping over the man and kicking the man's gun across the hall, he finally walked into the main room. There he held up the gun in both hands, pointed across the large area at an man who was rising from an over stuffed chair. The man was smart and froze as he saw the black specter moving into his apartment.

"Don't sit down because you need to get out of your clothes." In a deep voice, Damian yanked the silencer off the gun and let the man see the deadly hole pointing at him.

"My guys will be back soon and then you will die a slow and painful death." The man had an accent.

Moving slowly sideways, Damian reached what must be the dining area. He pulled the end chair that had arms and slowly drug it back, never letter the bore of the gun waver.

"I think they are going to be busy for a while following your orders and burning down that whore house. I think I told you to start getting out of those clothes. You won't like it if I do it." With his free hand, Damian reached down and pulled out a wicked looking knife about eighteen inches. At that type of urging the man kicked off his shoes and began to drop his pants. It took him a while to get out of everything except loose undershorts. Damian knew the man was wasting time on purpose and he let the man keep the ugly shorts.

"On the chair." Using the forty-five to point, Damian waited until the man sat down in the sturdy wooden chair then walked behind him and tapped him on the head once hard with the barrel of the gun. Having the man out for a while helped him get the man taped to the chair.

When the man woke up, he was duct tapped to the chair, arms and ankles against the frames and even around his chest and across his thighs. He realized he was not going to get out unless someone came and cut him loose. What he saw and smelled was this man in black with the dangerous grey eyes pouring gas from a can in a circle around on the floor where he sat unable to move.

The whole thing got worse when the asshole set the can down far across the room. He came back and standing about six feet away he brought out a plain Bic.

"I'm going to ask you a couple of questions and you're going to answer them."

"Fuck you." The man was angrier than he had been in a long time. He could think of a lot of ways to kill this bastard.

There was a click and then the idiot took to a heel and reached forward and lit the circle of gas. Suddenly the old man was in a circle of flames and even though it was not touching him, he felt the heat.

"Now about my questions, I know you are Artur DeMartu, but I want to know who you send tributes to? Who do you owe your allegiance?" Now the man in black stood. His ugly gun was lying over on the settee where Artur had been when this threat entered.

"You will die. We both will burn up together, you fuckin idiot." Artur flung some curses in his home language.

"Well, Artur. I have done my homework. I checked this building out. Your floor is thirty feet above the oil tank in the garage. Also, there is no extra flooring or ceiling under it. I wonder how long it is going to take that gas fire to burn through the wood and dump you, fire and all down on all that old oil below?" Now the threatening man picked up the gas can and moved it over towards the door he had entered. It was as if he was ignoring Artur.

"Hey, you mother fucker. How you going to put that fire out if I answer your questions?" Artur snorted and waited to see how the game played out. Inside he was beginning to worry as he saw the fire eating at the old wood.

"Well," Damian drew the word out as he stepped back closer. "I could find a fire extinguisher. But this old place lacks a lot of things. I could get some water from that small kitchen but I would have to run back and forth a lot of times. That doesn't seem very smart." Now the old man was seeing the flames reflected in the grey eyes. "But the easiest way would be to just reach in and pull you and the chair out of the circle. Yep, that sounds like the best way."

Now Artur looked around as far as his restricted movements would let him. The stranger in the dark garb was right, the man could pull him out of the circle. If there had ever been a fire extinguisher in this whole old garage it was past any use.

"What do you want to know?" Artur's accent was getting stronger along with his fear.

"Who do you owe your honor to and send your tributes?" Damian knew that in the old ways these men had a hierarchy way of status and that someone else was still in charge and handing out orders.

Waiting to think about his situation and what it was going to cost him, Artur watched the flames and felt the heat. His bare toes were beginning to be too hot and soon there would be blisters on his feet. Thinking that he might be dead in either way, he chose to live and try to appease his pater. For the next few moments, as heat hurt him, he told the man in black everything.

Artur gave names and places and even told where his private cell phone with all the contact numbers was hidden in the apartment. He gave the pass code for the small safe in the back room and then waited. Of course, the man had to check to make sure he wasn't lying so he suffered as the man went to retrieve the phone. He heard over the crackles of the old floor as the fire ate at it while the man opened the small safe and took the packets of money and small bag of diamonds.

When the dark figure came back into the room, his hands were empty. Evidently everything was stuffed into pockets in that military type black assassin type uniform. Then the work hit Artur. Assassin.

"Wait. I can pay you a lot more than whoever sent you to kill me. Let me go and you'll never hav'ta work agin'." Now he was pleading.

Picking up the can, Damian tilted it as he walked out of the room. He left a trail of gas down the hall, over the dead guard and down the stairs. He knew the flames around the old man would soon burst brighter as the air caught fumes. Now he began pouring the rest of the can around the garage, leaving the cans where ever they were empty. He heard the poof from upstairs and the flame filled the upper doorway.

Up to that point the old man had never stopped yelling. Artur screamed offers of funds and threats of death in two languages. He cussed in words that Damian never heard and then told of where some additional money could be found in this city. But the yells stopped with the flash over as the air was eaten by the flames.

His job done, he stepped outside and took off his gloves and vest and shoes and tossed them through the door in different directions so they didn't make a pile. He did make sure they all ended up on some wet gasoline. He changed clothes in the car, bundling all the black items into a tote that held his suit. Driving the sedan back to Station 12, he dropped it off and signed all the proper papers. By the time he reached his Charger, he had a call on his cell.

"Detective Walker? I'm Detective Romkowski. Chief Reede put me in charge of the clean up on a tip on a gang rumble at 12245 Monrose."

"Great. How's it going?"

"Well," Detective Romkowski sounded tired. "We ended up with a shoot out on both sides. I should have listened to the Chief and brought more guys. We have everyone rolling out now and it is under control. I guess you had info that this was a full on war."

"I did tell the Chief my CI said that all the Valducci gang was going out on a raid. Sorry if the full details didn't get relayed to you. Did any of ours get hurt?" Damian waited as he got the Charger out and on the street.

"Minimum. Are you coming over?"

"At this time, I thought I would go over past their hang out and see if anyone is still there. I might catch a couple still hanging around that has outstanding warrants. I'll check in later to see the reports. Good job, Romkowski."

By the time Damian got back to the garage it was in full bloom and there were two different divisions of fire stations with all their men, that had reported to the location.

Chapter Ten

Detective Damian Walker made a couple of stops before he got to the office the next night. He stopped for a coffee and snacks at the corner deli. He dropped a small bag of garbage from his car in the big container outside. It had the smell of piss and vomit, so no one was going to want to open the loose tie.

Once he pulled into the spot behind the tall building and parked in the Reserved spot that was not his to use, he pulled out another plastic bag and walked over to the back building. This was where the cars were worked on and other mechanical processes were done. Here also was where some items were tossed into an open area that would be handled with care and eventually burned.

He handed the black standard release bag to the cop on duty and signed all the forms. It was stated that it was only some debris that the firemen from last night's fire stated was not important.

"Yeah," Damian nodded. "All the important items are probably down in the basement with the lab guys sorting through them. You will get some more burn bags before everyone is done."

He was right, as after a fire that involved bodies, there was a lot of evidence to go through and the big black CSI trucks brought too much back with them. The first load of unwanted was sent out withing a couple of hours and would continue through the next few days. Damian's bag was just one among many that disappeared into the hot furnace that ate everything leaving no ashes.

At the end of the short meeting, he reported to the Chief that he had seen the gang hole burn down and even dropped off the usual stuff to be burned at the back before he came in to file reports.

"Come to my office for a minute." Reede took off down between an open aisle and desks back to where his office door was open.

Once Reede was behind his desk and in the large chair he had moved into the office, he asked Walker to close the door and take a seat.

"Great job on wiping out the Valducci gang." Reede pulled up some reports on his computer as he talked.

"All I did, Chief, was pass on the word. The guys on the streets and the SWAT teams did all the work."

"Yeah, yeah, yeah." Reede waved his hand to stop the Detective from saying anything more. "And being first at the fire was such a coincidence. Well, it isn't something that can go in your file, but I know someone who is cleaning up the streets. So in a quiet way, good job and keep it up. That is why I brought you in here."

He flipped his computer screen around and it showed a report on a list of recent deaths. They were the sort of people who lived on the streets or were the low-end kind of users who bought with their last dollar. They usually didn't have family and ended up buried in Potter's Field.

"Crime is like life, it hates a vacuum so it expands to fill up when it finds a hole."

Looking at the details of the death reports, Damian was seeing a report from the police medical examiner of a type of drug that was all tied together. Someone was bringing in a drug that was hitting the street in a clean heavy dose.

"What do you need, Chief?"

Turning the screen back around, Reede nodded. "I need

you to hit the street and get me some answers. You do that better than all the others in this station."

It was exactly the type of work that Detective Damian Walker lived for, being on his own and walking the streets late into the night. He could listen to the talk as pushers traded information and desperate buyers hunted for the quick hit.

Times had changed and so did the people. The music was Latin but not Mexican. The people had a different look about them. They were not as desperate and escaping from their homeland. They were coming north to get the gringos dollar.

As Damian came out of a dark alley to lean against a wall where no one would see him, he watched down the street. Even though it was almost three in the morning, the area was busy with young people walking from open bars with live guitar entertainment.

The English that was spoken had heavy accents for people from Columbia, Peru and Bolivia. But the ones that stood out with the best cars and the fancy silk shirts were the new ones from Honduras. This was the new importers that the DEA and others of the alphabet soup had not been able to stop the flow of the new drugs from that country.

Of course, the government boys were interested in catching the big boys back in South America and hopefully in a year or two stop the whole show. But while the local streets had people dying, the feds had no interest as they were blinded by what they called the big picture. Who was to judge?

But tonight, like the past couple and for the next few, Damian was watching and learning. He now had a car or two picked out that had someone in the back seat that never got out. The guy was young but gave orders but not drugs. He was smart enough to keep some distance between him and the pushers. But Damian knew the pushers had to get their supply somewhere. That was what he was hunting for and patience would pay off.

The guy giving orders rode in a SUV top of the line and all tricked out. Damian would bet it even had bullet proof windows behind all that dark tint.

The next car he was interested in was a low rider, new from Detroit and also with dark tinted windows. The guys that got out of this car were dressed different, loose clothes that were bright colors and mismatched with a lot of heavy jewelry.

Standing in the dark doorways and leaning against walls at the end of alleys, Walker listened and learned and watched. This was interesting and disgusting to dwell into the lives of crime.

Starting on the streets he found out that these men didn't use the sex shops. They did have some loose girls that they passed around but sex was always done in private, one on one. It might be in the car or behind a convenient door, but afterwards there was bragging.

These men did a lot of bragging, both in Spanish and English. They bragged when they drank, had sex, what they drove and raced and about their families. That was something else. These people set up a family life starting with the males at a young age.

There was a loose type of gang association that seemed to be based on homelands and tats. The Peruvians all were on one corner and the boys from other countries were scattered in groups on other streets. It was the tattoos that told the stories and what drew the interest. In these areas the tattoo parlors were open most of the night and all day. The fascination of getting a story told on the body was deep in these South American boys.

After night upon night of watching the streets with a different culture, Damian decided to move in closer. He also knew he would stand out as he was, a tall grey eyed gringo.

But he went into one of the bars full of the fast tempo music and sat at the end of the bar and left a big tip. He drank several tequila's straight up and finished the night with an Aquila beer. He didn't try to speak to anyone or pump the lady bartender for info. He just repeated his actions for five nights.

On the sixth night and group of four toughs with bandanas tied over their foreheads and enough gold chains to open their own store walked around him. One took the open seat beside him and one leaned on the end of the bar and the other two were behind him.

Yet what these puffed up bullies didn't notice is that he only had one hand up on the bar, holding the can of beer. The bartender always brought the cold can over and opened it, but never offered to pour it into a glass. This beer from Columbia was meant to be taken from the imported tin.

"Yo in the wrong part of town, tall man." The guy on the stool leaned in and breathed garlic.

Slowly Damian took a long sip of the beer and then set it carefully on the tab the bartender had placed earlier. "Not if I want to get a good beer." He kept his voice low.

"I think you better change your taste in brew and go to the other side of town to drink." The guy was making a ton of mistakes. He was too close. He had a small gun, tilted sideways in Damian's ribs and he was looking over at his buddies with a big gold tooth grin instead of watching the mark. Yep, he did it all wrong.

Pushing the beer can back a little further out of the way, Damian took a deep breath and the action was quick. Not having to use his own big gun, Damian reached out and with both hands had the kid's gun, clamping the guy's fingers inside and then with a twist the kid was pinned.

Looking on helpless, the three buddies stepped back as they watched and heard their friend screaming in pain. His hand was twisted backwards, caught in the gun, one finger inside the guide but unable to pull the trigger. That was good, because now the barrel was pointed at his own forehead and the pain in his hand was merciless. His head was pinned back against the bar and his feet there splayed out trying to keep him upright on the stool.

Standing with his long legs straddling his own stool, Damian waited a moment to see if any of the others were going to act. But the idiots who were yelling in Spanish louder than the one he had pinned, were backing away.

Leaning into the crying kid who had his own gun aimed at his eye, Daimon spoke into his ear. "Shut up and tell them to quit talking or you will pull the trigger and kill yourself." The grip on the hand that had trapped the kid's own hand within the trigger guard of the pistol tightened and the kid actually had tears.

But he did yell out and the room got quiet, the whole room. Even the bartender froze at the other end. She was probably trying to decide to reach for a shotgun or run. She was smart and it looked like she had an eye on the back door.

"Now I want to finish my beer and I want to come back here again to drink and not get bothered. When I leave go of your hand, I think I should buy you a drink to help your pain that you caused yourself. You do remember that you are the one who made the mistake here right?" Damian was speaking so low and close to the punk, that he was pushing the head band upward. But he wanted the conversation to be private.

The el maton understood he had a chance to live and even gain some credit for all this. "I, I need a drink."

Taking the greasy pistol as he pulled the hand around, Damian placed the kid's gun on the bar and helped him turn around to sit on the stool. Damian sat down on his and with their backs to the three amigos, Damian waved at the bartender who still had not moved.

"Two Casamigos Blanco." Daimon laid a couple of

hundred's on the bar and his accent was perfect when he said the name of the tequila.

"You know that is an okay pistol but I carry a heavier one." Damian pulled out the big slugger and the lights reflected off the chrome. He was giving time to let the kid act like a man and start to show off in front of his friends.

Laying the two guns side by side, the difference also said something about the two men. But the detective was giving the street crook a chance to recover and even show off after the fiasco of the take down.

With his back to everyone, the kid used the sleeves on his fancy shirt to wipe his face as he reached for the big gun.

"What is it?"

"It's called a Magnum Research Desert Eagle 50 Action Express. And its big, so it is good to hold it in two hands."

Picking up the beautiful deadly weapon, the kid felt all his power return. He slowly turned with the shiny power and faced the three others with the matching bandanas tied on their heads and special tats on their wrists. By this time the two guitarists had started to play again and people were moving.

The bartender was reaching into a deep ice bin for the special brew and things had almost returned to normal for such a place. She bought the two drinks in ice cold glasses and Damian took his first sip. It was like swallowing ice that began to turn to fire half way down to the stomach. By the time it settled and hit the brain the world was tilted.

By the end of the night, or should the term be morning, Damian had some new friends, an expensive bottle of booze was gone and there was two holes in the outside wall of the bar. Thankfully the bullets had not hit anyone.

Gus, Raf and JoJo had pledged to meet him in a few nights at this same place and that was even after he showed them the gold shield. They thought it was something to brag about to their porch groups, that they had an in with the cops. It gave them rank.

For Damian, it allowed him to walk the night streets and not draw a lot of attention. He was starting to blend in with some of the beggars and those who belonged here, but were not Hispanic.

Walking the streets at night did not solve the problems of crime. The Chief was right, take out one problem and it left a hole that was soon to be filled. Human nature created good and bad. But this problem with the drugs on the streets and the small crimes committed by the South American gangs was different.

For one, Walker decided that there was no central group or top boss that could wipe out the whole problem. This was a constant influx of new faces, mixing in with the established or setting up new forces. The problem was the drugs. Stop the flow of drugs from Honduras to these individuals and they would either leave or settle down as families and residents.

The big problem was that they were only city police, and there was no way they could affect the next state let alone another country. But there had to be an entry point for the drugs in their own area, so for the next few weeks, visiting with Gus, Raf and JoJo and amigos, or walking the dark alleys, Damian watched and listened.

It was like being a little boy lost in the forest. He had the training of his scout leader experience. He had to find a small stream and follow it to find where it poured into a larger one. Keep that up and the boy would find a river, and if he built a raft he would find an ocean.

So, there were fancy cars that appeared every few nights. The delivery trucks to the bars and delis made regular trips, some nightly and others weekly. There were the news trucks with the papers for the corner boxes and the stands for magazines and everything else. Once he began to watch, there was a lot of movement on these quiet dark streets.

Tracing back the streams, only two sets of trucks led back to rivers. The news trucks had to go back to the loading dock of the newspaper houses. There large trucks brought in loads of all type of stock besides the big rolls of paper. The liquor deliveries had to return to the storage warehouses, where semis brought in shipments from everywhere, especially overseas. Bingo.

Starting at the stream, he bought some good stuff from the bartender. It was easy and the lab boys in the basement said it had only been halved with backing powder, but was good Honduran. He went to the meeting at the next shift. He had missed most for months but stayed after to walk with Reede to the Chief's office.

"Boss, to wipe out the gang problem in the Hispanic sector, I need one hundred and twenty K of unmarked bills.?" Detective Damian Walker went right to the issue.

"It's cheaper to burn down a couple of buildings." The Chief sat back in his chair and looked at his best man. He was referring to what had happened to the Valducci gang.

"Yep," Walker leaned back against the wall. He didn't have a jacket on and everyone saw the unusual weapon and extra clips that he wore in his special made holster. "But the feds won't let us burn down a foreign country, so we have to buy our way out of this one. Oh, there might be one large explosion."

With a chuckle, Reede began to type in his computer. "I don't trust many people. It will be ready by the time you get to the cashier. You could send me a note now and then to let me know what to expect," he raised his eyebrows. "or not."

Walker nodded and left.

Chapter Eleven

Doing what he did best, he relaxed and spent hours in the dark alley behind the bar, watching the different delivery trucks. There was one beer truck that went in with his trolly and then came back out to his cab and got another beer case that he carried inside.

After watching this done twice, a week apart, Damian sat on the foot step by the truck door and waited for the driver to return. The driver came out with a clip board and his head down. He was almost face to face as Damian stood up.

"Hey, you surprise me. I have no extra deliveries tonight." The man gave a large grin, showing a lot of white teeth.

"I want a special delivery. The type you make in the back room of the bar. Only larger."

The driver shook his head even though he kept the smile. "Sorry, I don't have any extra beer on board."

"I'm looking for something better than beer." Damian pulled his coat open wide to reach in and grab a couple of bands of bills. He also showed that he had more of the bills in bundles in the pocket. Throwing open the coat allowed the driver to see both his big weapon and the gold shield on his belt.

The driver's reaction was strange.

"Oh, Bless the Holy Virgin. You're the dirty cop that the cábula have all been bragging about. My Gods it so good to meet you." The driver grabbed Damian's hand and was pumping it furiously as if he had a jack under his truck and was lifting the whole side.

"I am Carlos Munez and it is an honor to be in your presence. I will only tell the correct hombre." Now he still grinned largely but pulled the detective over to the side. "Wait, I will get you a cold one."

With that he opened the door and stepped up to reach across the driver's seat. Damian could hear him shuffling something and began to close his hand around the big handle of the special weapon in the holster. But the guy stepped back down with two glass bottles of beer.

"I always carry cold ones in a chest. No one counts all the boxes that are delivered." He hit the cap on the edge of the open door and held out the open bottle.

Taking a long slug from the bottle, Walker sat it down on the step and then finally pulled out the wad of bills that equaled twenty thousand. "I need some Honduran Gold."

"Oh, great. That's a nice buy. My seller will like that. When?" The stupid driver was slugging his beer and grinning even larger.

"As soon as I can meet your seller."

"Oh, that's not good." The driver drained his bottle and shook his head. He still grinned. "My seller is my personal secret."

"Hmm," Damian reached into his obvious money stash and pulled out two more large packs. "How about I make it worth your while? You don't even have to share to tell anyone, especially your seller."

An agreement was met with a lot of hand shaking and grins. Damian refused to ride in the truck which is what the driver requested. But the big truck was easy to follow as this was his last stop. So it was over several blocks, down to the docks on the river and parking outside an office across from all the warehouses.

The idea was for Damian to wait in his car while the beer diver went in and talked to his seller. As far as the detective was concerned this driver had to be one of the dumbest distributors on the streets. He had just given Damian the location of the next guy up the chain of distribution.

For now, he would play the game and wait for an introduction. It was almost forty-five minutes before the diver appeared at the door and waved for him. Damian got out of the car and went over to join the man who was still grinning. This man had taken happy pills earlier.

"Mr. Ortez is busy and might be a bit short, so keep to the subject."

For this happy guy to make a warning meant that the seller probably was not in a good mood. Walker's guess was right, as he was ushered through the front empty office into the back one, a man sat at a desk. On the flat surface in front of him was a Glock. The man was wearing a dark dress shirt and had a jacket on the chair behind him. There were two battered metal file cabinets in one corner, but the window was boarded over.

There was one stiff metal chair in front of the desk that the driver shifted indicating that Damian should sit down.

"So, my guy says you want a big buy. Why not get it from him?" At these words, the driver put the twenty thousand on the corner of the table.

"He offered this for a bigger buy, Mr. Ortez." The grin was there as the guy backed out of the room.

"Ya' dinna' want to wait for my guy to bring you such an order. Or did you think he would cut it?" The guy leaned forward and put his hands on both sides of the black gun.

"Actually, I'll take this buy. But I need a larger amount." Damian swung his coat open on both sides, showing the chrome of his big weapon on one side and the bulge of wrapped bills on the other. "I want to set up for a regular large movement through the police station. I and a couple of other guys have a way of moving loads in impound cars. I'm not going into details, but this shield is gold for Detective so you're not messing with some street black and white." Now he sat back and waited.

"How much? The guy was interested.

"A hundred K on the first buy to test the quality and movement. The next one would be five times that." Damian waited for the guy to do the math. Mr. Ortez was not multiplying five times one hundred thousand, he was figuring his share of each transaction. Like all drug pushers, it was all about the money that stayed in their own pocket. Unlike the driver Mr. Ortez did not smile, but his face did show appreciation.

"I will have to talk to my provisioner to set up such a larger supply. When are you looking for delivery?"

"I need to meet with your provisioner. I won't deal through a middleman on such a large amount on a regular basis. Of course, you will still get a bonus on each transaction." Damian spoke low and firm. He wanted to get the message into the brain of this Mr. Ortez.

"No. Everything goes through me. The next level doesn't meet with anyone else." Now the man sat back and frowned.

Watching him, Damian decided to give the man the bait. "Okay. I will see if I can find out if the Peruvians are interested in moving some larger shipments."

CHAPTER TWELVE

In the low car, the Detective was following a tricked-out Caddy SUV that had Mr. Ortez sitting in the back seat. He had a driver and a shot gun guard. Actually, no shotguns, just forty-fives.

The trip was short as it was only a few blocks past the warehouses and down to the area where the big docks were located. There were storerooms and garages and offices set back behind the many shipping containers.

In small letters on a window that was blacked out the name said Guaranteed Shipping, Inc. M. Gustavos, Manager. Everyone parked and got out of their vehicles with no weapons showing. One of the lackey's held the door open, so the Detective followed Mr. Ortez into what was a large open room with a lot of crates along one wall and a couple of desks on the other.

Among some cabinets and small stacked crates that divided the area was another desk with some people that Damian could not see. It was indicated that he was to wait by the front desk with the two jerk guards while Mr. Ortez went to the back.

After a few moments he came forward, following a woman. As she got closer, Damian had to remember to breath. Every eye in the place, male and female turned to watch the woman walk towards the front of the unofficial office.

For the first time since he was a child, he was seeing a sight that mesmerized and surprised him. She was the most beautiful woman he had ever seen. Oh, there were beautiful woman on TV and in the movies, but everyone knew they had a lot of make up on and special lighting and hair had been touched up.

On the streets, he had witnessed a lot of lovely women in the sex shops, some he was surprised that they stooped so low. In the bars and hotel lobbies were the high-priced pros that went over a thousand or more a night. But this Madonna was above par over any angel that had come down to walk before the eyes of man.

He was tall at six foot one, but her long legs put her at five foot nine or ten. Yet it wasn't the legs, or the great hips or the full breast, it was the long neck up to the perfect face that even the Renaissance artists could not have created. Framed in a cascade abundance of jet-black hair that matched the arched eyebrows over extra large dark eyes. Eyes that were surrounded by long lashes that didn't detract from the whites that were pure.

A pedigree nose with high clean cheekbones that held only a touch of blush drew attention to the strong clean lines of a jaw bone that begged to be kissed. But strongest of all were the full lips, the top not too large and the bottom brimming in red color.

A flat forehead without wrinkles didn't give away an age, but the Detective felt that the way she moved and carried herself, that she might be closer to his forty years.

Mr. Ortez was starting to introduce them but he stumbled both over his feet and tongue. "Um,"

At this point the man hit the side of a cabinet as he was watching the woman and not where he was walking. Catching himself, he mumbled something in Spanish and then straighten up.

"Detective this is Melorosha Gustavos."

She stopped and frowned at Ortez and put a lovely smile

on Damian. "Sorry, Detective. I didn't get your full name."

Trying to get back on track, he nodded. "My pleasure Madame Gustavos. It is Damian Walker. Can we sit and talk about a future deal?"

"Please, call me Mel." She turned and led the way back. He looked at all that hair and then his eyes were locked on those hips. But he fought to get his mind back into his own body. So far, the trail of drug supply was only a list of dead bodies in the near future to stop the Hondurans in his city. But how did you kill perfection?

If Mel was the one receiving the packages from the high guy in the beautiful mountains of Middle America, then she was the next on the list to stop. Fuck.

Her desk was full but neat, with everything in piles or stack trays. There wasn't a land phone, but he would bet she had a cell on her somewhere. They were left alone even though there were people all over doing different jobs. Some were moving crates and a couple were doing some type of office work, using portable computers.

Since he wasn't sure he could make his mouth work right, he asked her to give him a run down on her business and her ties to Honduras. He made a mistake and watched those lips and sometimes didn't hear the words. But some began to settle through and he had an idea of what was behind this particular line of drug movements.

There was a relative back home that was either a Senator or in tight with the government. There were large mountain ranches protected by the military where the crops were raised and everything was processed.

Since Honduras wasn't really part of the large continent of South America and was south of the problems of the big country of Mexico, it was mostly ignored by the US and most importantly the DEA. She was pleased to share this general knowledge with the local dirty cop.

She also shared that although though there area there were many cops on the take, he was the first Detective. But she did list the ones inside the courts, jails and records. He had no way of recording any of this, but if he could get her out of his mind for a few minutes, he would put it all down later.

Next, she explained that the top guy back in little Honduras had six of his so called family set up over the United States, all in situations like hers. That exquisite mouth of hers spelled out the whole picture thinking she was winding in the dirty cop.

She thought of using this cop for inside information and would make a good deal with him. He thought about getting her long legs around him with both of them naked. No, wipe that away. She was the mogul that needed to be eliminated to clean up his streets. Fuck.

It was almost dawn before she was called away for other business and he went out to his car. It was too late to make any type of report to the Chief so Walker decided to go home and put everything together that was rattling around in his head and lower.

The next night's shift he was early and sat through the whole meeting and all of the announcements. He probably looked like hell as he had gotten little rest and almost no sleep rolling in his bed. His rough several days old beard added to the appearance of spending too much time in the bars.

Once in the office, Damian slumped into the chair and watched the Chief shut the door and go around the desk. Reede punched the phone to shut it off and allow him to ignore all incoming calls.

"Report." As usual the Chief wasted few words and went right to the point.

Scooting over his police pad that was metal encased, Damian let the Chief take his time and scan through the recap first of the Detectives work over the past weeks.

After a half hour the older man looked up. "So, what do you feel about the Hispanic community?"

"They are entirely different from the Valducci situation. The Europeans that were involved in the gangs and drugs were here alone and had families back in what they called the old country. They had no allegiance to anyone or anything but themselves and the money.

But the Hispanics are different. They have moved here to stay. They keep a portion of the drug money to keep themselves more comfortable. They have families that they take care of and enjoy the kids. A large part of the street guys are even religious, with the church busy on special holidays.

They have gangs, but a family is more important than a gang member. Plus, they don't use the sex shops. They don't pick up the pros who work the corners. They have a few girls that they pass around and they show off.

They brag about their sexual powers and about their weapons. They wear colors and tats to mark who they are and they like gold. By that I mean, gold teeth, gold jewelry and the bigger the better. They also like cars which is hard to park or storage in legal garage areas in our busy city. A car is a status symbol."

Reede slid the special pad back across the desk. "What happens when the drug supply stops for all of the local Hispanics in our area?"

With a chuckle, Damian tapped a picture. It showed a dark-skinned young man and a pretty dark eyed woman holding the hands of a child between them as they walked. "Chief, we have a lot of new citizens."

"So, we not only need to shut down the show at the river docks, but we need to do more?" Reede asked the question hoping his favorite Detective had an answer.

"Oh, shit yes. I have one real strong answer. But you don't want to know about it and I'm not sure I'm up to doing it."

Walker had a look of despair that didn't fit on the tall man's face. Was it possible to fall in love at first sight like in the romance stories?

"Tell me everything and how many people you need?" If there was one thing that Damian respected, was Reede's ability to make quick and firm decisions. The idea was to wait until the next shipment came up the river and was unloaded. That gave Walker about eight days or nights to be exact, to come up with a way of how to handle the situation with Mel.

Waiting two nights, he stayed away from the Hispanics and the dock area. He walked his old area and even stopped in to visit with a couple the sex shops to get the latest update on the streets. It was all about the Honduran Gold that everyone was using. The problem was that a lot of it was too pure and there were seventeen deaths and the hospitals were full of over doses. These people needed the old stuff that was hard to get and was cut several times as it passed down the stream.

Looking to the future, Walker had a lot of years ahead of him before retirement, if he chose that route. He could always end up like the Chief, growing old on the job.

At last, he tooled the Charger over and pulled up in front of Guaranteed Shipping, Inc. M. Gustavos, Manager. This time there was a big guy with a long coat pretending to be standing around smoking. Damian bet the heavy coat covered a long automatic.

"I'm here to make a deposit." Walker was smart enough not to reach for the door knob, but he tilted his hat back so the camera would show his face. There was a beep and the punk reached and opened the door for him.

Walking through the strange warehouse office, this time he made his way to the back and Mel's desk. No one stopped him but all eyes were on her as she walked in those tall heels to meet him. She affected him the same way, an angel who grabbed his breath and alerted his cock.

"Well, handsome. You look better with the hat back." She was referring to the fact that his hat was tilted back.

He reached into his pocket and pulled out one of the flat zippered blue bank bags. "I have the fifty K. That is the first half. You can count it."

Waving for a worker to take the bank envelope, she smiled. "I don't count money. No one would be foolish enough to give me the wrong amount. Have you eaten?" With these words she turned and seemed to expect him to follow. Like a lonely puppy, he did as expected.

They wandered back past office workers, warehouse and maintenance people and guards. All eyes were on her including Damian's as he watched the soft sway of her hips. Could he really eliminate this body from the world?

Getting to the back, there was a door that some guy hurried over to open for them. Outside in the dark, they were escorted across the dark alley to the back door of another building. One of the guards held it open for her, so Damian went in behind her to find themselves in a side passage of a kitchen area for a restaurant.

Of course, all the helpers looked up and watched her walk through to push on a two way door and go out into the dining room. At this time of night, Walker was surprised to find the place almost full.

Mel went immediately over to a booth that was close to where they came out, but had privacy. It didn't take long for a waiter to bring a tray that held two glasses of water and two matching ones that held the right color. This lady like good whiskey and this place took good care of her and her guests.

"Your usual, Miss Mel?" The waiter stood at ease but held the tray behind him.

"No, Al. Two of your best pork chops tonight, with all the usual fixings."

"I'll have the chef right on it, Miss Mel." With that he was gone but soon returned with some salsa and chips. Then he disappeared and the two had some time to talk.

As she took a chip and dipped it into the home made salsa, Damian noticed something important. On that right hand, encircling the first or pointing finger was a large elaborate ring. It was silver in color, but from how involved it was, he thought it probably was platinum. A lot of filigree had been created in a heavy pattern that created a single G which must have stood for the Gustavos family. In the center was an impressive round Opal. He did remember that some of the finest Opals in the world came from the mines of Honduras.

"That is really an impressive ring. It seems a bit large for such a beautiful lady." Walker picked up his whiskey to allow him to watch her eyes over the rim as he sipped. He had to do something to keep his eyes off those lips.

"It's a family thing. Each of the cousin's here in the US has one. You have a large ring too." She also took a sip of the good whiskey.

Damian decided she didn't want to discuss her family, but he already had an idea besides taking the life of this divine female. He decided a different track.

"If you hadn't gone into the family business, what would you have done?" He watched those eyes.

"Wow, you are the strange one. I expected this conversation to be about how you could get my price down." Mel shook all that mess of soft hair back and looked around. Perhaps she didn't want anyone hearing her talking about her personal life.

"Well, Mr. Cop. I originally had plans to go to college. I have a friend who came up here and finished college. She now lives in Canada. Our lives are very different."

Now he tried a chip and dipped into the red sauce. "Would you trade places with her if you could?"

Mel's laugh was brittle. "I quit believing in fairy tales when

I had my first period. Is there a good Detective out there somewhere that you would change places with, Mr. Cop?"

Thinking of that question, Damian wondered if he was a good or bad Detective. He did things that would get him in the gas chamber of this state, but he felt each time he stepped over that line, he went home and slept without nightmares.

At last, the food came and the conversation stopped.

Chapter Thirteen

There wasn't much talk once the food came. Mel got a couple of calls and there was some price and delivery discussion. There was no dessert and she rushed off, telling him to take his time to finish and leave when he was done. Mel told him the meal was on her.

Not wanting to walk through the office that belonged to Mel, he went out the front of the restaurant and took his time walking around the long street and marked off driving area to where his car was parked. The long walk in the fog muddled his mind but made a few things clear to him. It seemed he was about to bite off a lot more than any man could hope to chew. Why not play it the simple way and eliminate all the working people who could move this particular deal? But there needed to be a message sent back to the factory in Honduras so that it did not get started up again in this city.

For the next few nights, Damian had many projects to watch over. First there was working with each Detective that had been assigned to each take down. These people also worked in different rooms on different floors where they each met with types of SWAT teams that would be part of the action. The orders from the Chief were to take alive if possible but to take no chances and no questions would be asked.

At the bar they needed her right hand first finger and her positive ID, perhaps her Driver's License or Permit for working as a bartender. The same instructions were given to the group that was going to handle the delivery man. Two groups would take down everyone at Guaranteed Shipping, Inc. It would be hit from the front and back and SWAT dropped by helicopters on the roof. They had discreetly checked out and found two openings on the top of the building.

The instructions direct from the Chief was to take the right hand first finger and a proper ID, dead or alive.

Keeping an eye on everything and filling in details, Damian began to spend some time with Mel. They were the odd fellows of the system and that drew them together. He needed to keep in contact with her to mark her movements. It also led up to him knowing her better to reach his final decision. Could he eliminate her or save her? How deep was she into the family business?

There came a time when she indicated him to follow her, and while all eyes were on her graceful movements as they moved out the back door. But this time they didn't go across to the back door of the restaurant. Mel walked down the alley, across and narrow intersection and part way down to another building. There she entered and climbed a set of stairs. At the top was another of one of her guards who nodded and held a door open for her.

Following her in, he stopped immediately when he heard the door close behind him. Standing there he looked around a large area and realized he was in her apartment. To say it was unusual would be an understatement. It was an open design, taking in the whole second floor of about eighty square feet.

His eyes were drawn to one wall that was all windows looking out on the distant docks letting in the lights from the wharves and the ships and workers. Looking for the important items, he found the king size bed off to his right deep in a dark corner surrounded by polished wooden chests and cabinets.

There were four stanchions quartering the large area that had to be part of the construction of the building. Around one was a freestanding kitchen area. That made since these rectangular posts that held up everything would also hold lots of wiring and pipes.

Taking off from another was were etched glass walls that it took him a while to understand. It was later in the evening before he discovered this was a bathroom of imagination that opened to the side where the bed was displayed.

Off near the windows in a place that took up more room than his apartment was a complex seating arrangement. Using that fourth upright post as a back, the elaborate media set up was attached and supported with a long chest below with too many gadgets for him to name.

As the lights slowly came on around the big apartment, everything was subtly lit to let the entire room be seen and used. There were thick rugs and the colors were mostly white or beige. It might be large and open, but it was a place for a woman.

One thing was important to Damian, it was very different from anything connected with her business. There were no file cabinets, no loose files or papers lying around on any of the tables, cabinets or counters. The open shelves that he could see, seemed to hold either magazines or hard bound books.

"Find a seat in the TV area and I will get us both a drink." Mel had kicked off those painful very high heels and walked barefoot to the kitchen area. He was comfortable taking her word in the open design as he could watch her in the kitchen as he dumped his hat and coat on one chair and took another.

The whiskey was better than good and they sat and for a while he let her ask him questions. Most of them he could answer truthfully as they were about his childhood. Somewhere she began to talk about her own childhood and it had been good until her dad died in some type of work connected with her uncle.

Her mom started doing work for the so called family in some warehouse packing drugs and she played with some cousins. This was her introduction to the future with no choice. The few friends she had from school treated her with respect, but would not get close. Most of them acted as if they were afraid of her and her cousins.

The whiskey kept being poured and the talk slowed down, and they moved close together and somewhere there was contact. All the moves were mutual and he was grateful the rug was thick and soft and warm.

Damian couldn't remember exactly when or where all the clothes disappeared, but in the soft light when he saw those gorgeous orbs in the color of mocha, he knew he would never drink his coffee black again.

As he worked his tongue down a body that called to be worshiped, he heard her voice give him the noise he desired. Small pants of pleasure and slight gasps of special hits were what he heard. Then he found that rare nub that had only been gifted to females, so sensitive that his own tongue could bring her to the top of extasy. He heard her moans and felt the tremor of her release and knew that she was ready for him. Moving up and sliding slowly into that warm envelope was another trip to heaven.

Before then night was over, they had found another rug and ended up on the king size bed. Each move brought organisms and sweet sweat to both partners. At last, lying together against the pile of pillows, too tired to even sleep, they both were still together.

Lying on his back and admitting to himself that the lady had exhausted him, he felt her hand across his chest.

"Mel, what would you give to change your life and be like your friend in Canada?"

In a soft sleepy voice, Mel moved her hand. "Everything."

On the second night of strenuous but enervating love,

Damian asked the question again and then offered more. "What would you miss if you left all of this?"

"Nothing." Although the voice was soft and tired it was firm.

After a couple of more nights of planning with the teams back at the police station, Damian again had a night free to spend with Mel. By now the agreement was that he would send a text to a cell that she had, and if she responded they met at her apartment. It was an all clear and this night he finally made the proposal.

This time their love making had a companion. Under his pillow was the Magnum Research Desert Eagle 50 Action Express 6in Polished Chrome Pistol. He knew he was leaving her apartment with her right hand first finger that held the family ring or her life. He said a rare prayer, since he hadn't said a one since a kid.

The next night was complete chaos in the entire area for all the streets and blocks around the Hispanics and the docks. Police and SWAT teams came in larger groups than anyone had ever seen before.

Chief Reede had called on favors from other departments across the city and everyone was happy to be part of this raid. To close out a supply of one type of drug was too good a chance to miss.

By dawn the streets were back to normal. Some people were shocked, but a lot of locals were back in business. There had been many arrests of the gangs on the streets, but they would soon be back out with their families. There were some businesses that had been closed down and gaps in deliveries, but it would not take long for holes to be plugged. Life moved on for everyone, everywhere in the city.

In another part of the world life was different. It took ten weeks for Senor Rafaelo Gustavos, who was on his ranch to receive word that there was something important that needed his attention. It had to do with a ship that was on hold and had returned from the US. It was sitting in the port of La Ceiba.

It took something of great importance to get the rich businessman to make the trip to the port, but he had been told it involved a shipment that valued about two point four US million dollars. It was enough to get him and guards into four protected vehicles and make the four hour drive to the busy port.

Once they got to the right ship that had been cordoned off by his own people, Senor Gustavos demanded a clean nearby restroom. Several of his men went off in search and one was secured. When he returned, he indicated he was ready to board the freighter.

Chapter Fourteen

On the loading deck of the large freighter, the big bay doors were open. Two crates had been brought up and sat on the deck, but were now each covered with canvas.

Surrounded by his special team who spread out to make a large protective circle, Senor Gustavos walked up to the Captain who gave a slight bow.

The Captain made a motion and two seamen removed the tarp off of one of the crates. It had the top wood off and sitting against it and was open to be inspected. The breeze blew some loose wood shavings. The businessman knew what he was seeing. It was the way they packed the paper wrapped drugs with the wood chips around them to hide the smell and make a cushion. But when he got closer, he got a strong smell, one he had smelled earlier in the restroom. It was urine.

Walking around to stay a few feet away from the stink of the crate, he moved so that he could read the label on the top. It had a giant red stamp in English that said: RETURN TO SENDER.

Gustavos didn't have to get too close to the opening of the bay below to get the heavy scent of urine that was coming from the crates below. Everything was ruined and useless. Now he turned to face the other box that was still covered by a canvas.

Without even a motion, the seamen removed the tarp and exposed that there was a small box taped to the top of this unit. All that was on it was the name of Rafaelo Gustavos.

"Open it." Rafaelo Gustavos orders were in Spanish. But

his men began to move him back in case it was a bomb. The box didn't blow up, but it did make one of the men rush to the side of the ship to throw up. It held three fingers with heavy smears of dried blood all over the inside of the box. The only thing that was visible were the ID's and a flat ring on one finger and a very large elaborate ring on another.

In his familiar language Rafaelo requested that the fancy ring be cleaned and brought to him.

"There is no message, Sir."

"You are wrong. The message is very clear. Where was this entire shipment headed?" Now the businessman brought a clean white folded handkerchief to his nose.

"Senor, it was destined for all stops on the US River called the Mississippi. The plan was to go as far north as the draft of the ship allowed and dock to unload first delivery, then to stop on the way back to unload at other river ports. After first confrontation and damage and smell, we returned home." It was the Pilot who was nervously standing behind the Captain.

There was silence for a few minutes and then the Captain got brave and spoke.

"Senor. We can dump this mess and clean the ship to be ready to make another trip up the same river in forty-eight hours."

"No." Rafaelo Gustavos was not stupid and a very smart businessman. He picked his battles and knew how to accept a loss as part of running a family and a large company. "Clean up everything and get ready for another load. But it will not be our finest as we are between harvests. You will not go up that big river again. I think there is a nice port called Tampa and I will make some contacts with a trucking firm. Moving crates overland in the US is easy."

So, the world went on. People that used drugs never seemed to learn or resist. There were so many willing to take advantage of the weak, especially weak in their habits and needs.

For one man, a Detective of the police force in a city on the north link of the old Mississippi River, it all added to being out on the streets late at night. He remembered for a moment sitting in the low Dodge Charger, across from the small Trailways Office and watching as a few people got on the bus.

A father and a sleepy child left suitcases on the sidewalk for the driver to put in the low underneath hold. Then they followed the one other passenger. It was a female in bulky cargo pants, boots and a heavy padded jacket. She also left a rolling luggage cart for the driver, but had on a backpack. She had a billed hat on and even the hood of her inside sweater pulled up over her head. In the dark it was impossible to see her face or get any identification. He didn't need one. He was here to say good-bye to Mel.

But this was a different night, and he was out on the street alone, walking and watching. It was a quiet night as he walked slowly down an alley alone. Even the sex shops were without customers as one door stood open, a lady stepped into the opening to smell the fog and see the empty street. It was past midnight and things were waiting to happen.

Pulling up to the side of the street to get out his cell and answer the low tone, it was a text from his favorite Pathologist.

'We have another one. You need to see.'

Turning the Charger, it didn't take him long to pull around to the back of the large police building. Parking in the wrong zone he went immediately to the basement and through the halls to the morgue. Going past all the different working and storage areas, he turned into the unit were Jean worked. She had a man on a table under the bright lights that it appeared she was working on as she was in full garb looking like an astronaut. The city and especially Station 12 had a good working budget for this section and they had all the latest equipment.

"Detective, sorry you didn't get the call. The photos are over on the back wall." Jean began to remove her hood.

The CSI team did do a great job with all the different views of the body. Damian shook his head as he knew he had seen this same scene before. A beautiful woman laid out with her hands crossed over her chest. If you didn't look too close, you saw a tricked out pro with tight sexy clothes and even the lacy bra peeking. Heels that were too high and toes and fingers painted in bright red.

Her hair was clean and brushed back, but her face had on too much make-up especially around the closed eyes. Heavy blue shadow and fake long lashes painted black were accented by drawn in arched eyebrows.

But his instincts saw all the errors. This was a healthy, well nourished woman without any traces of miss use except what had happened to her that led to her death. Someone or maybe a group was out there as a serial killer and needed to be stopped.

"Want to take a first look?" Jean called him over to the table as she was about to prepare the victim. He stepped to the opposite side, but would move back out of the way when Jean worked. She had a large rolling cart with a box full of plastic collection bags for all items needed for forensics.

"Shoes don't fit." Jean carefully removed the shoes and placed them in a bag and sealed it. As the Pathologist went through her job carefully, Damian did not help as she rolled the body from side to side to get the clothes removed.

At last, with a nude body, Jean put a double filter in the drain and ran cold water over the body and hair. Then with the light that surrounded the large magnifying glass, she began her first examination.

"Yep, the usual bondage. I bet I get some fur in the catch drain from the padding on the cuffs." She had long needles where she would draw fluids for examination before she opened the body.

"Any special questions, Damian?"

"No, damn it. This is identical to the others. Thanks for letting me know. Do your job and I need to get out on the streets and do my thing." With that it didn't take him long to walk back out through the bright cold halls. He was so grateful when he sank into the leather of the Charger in the dark parking zone.

Pulling up the fancy heavy small portable computer, he got into the reports of the crime scene for the recent girl. Once he had the location he drove over to the address and was not surprised to find cop cars still there and yellow tape. He had stopped on the way to get two coffees, one with cream.

After parking and getting out, he set the cups on top of his car as he took the time to put his fedora on and open his long jacket to show the gold shield on his belt. He walked up to the officer who was leaning against the black and white, stuck on boring duty.

The coffee made it easy to stand and talk and look around. The scene was the same. Walker could see without moving away from the police car and by looking over the yellow tape where the body had been found. There were still the white outlines on the sidewalk and street that outlined where she had lain.

Glancing over he saw the open door of a small sex shop, but there was no one looking out, perhaps uncomfortable with cops so close. The killer or killers wanted to tie the body to sex and sluts, but Damian didn't buy it.

That was when an idea blossomed inside him. It was two people. There was one who enjoyed the BDSM scene and was a complete DOM. A person, probably a man since in most of those places and settings it was rare for a female DOM. That meant that the partner hated the victim. Someone who couldn't stand a clean-cut girl whose life was centered on getting some training or schooling and making plans for a good life. The pair took complete control and advantage when they came across the target and used her to their own warped needs.

The one for the domination of complete sex in all ways possible without a safe word. The other to kill the used girl and clean and paint and dress her as a slut. When she hadn't been raped in the mouth a ball gage had been too tight inside her mouth, because when the make-up was removed, the marks were on her face. The marks of her strangulation were also on her neck by a thick rope as it had been on all the others.

Moving away from the death scene and walking slowly down the street, he dumped the last of his coffee in the curb and pushed the paper cup down between the grills of the corner drain. This shop was not one where he went in much except to make a couple of arrests. He wasn't sure who the head receiver of funds was, but it didn't cause much trouble. Locally everyone knew the dead girl was not one of theirs.

What Damian knew was that he was looking for two people that liked to hurt innocent girls. Two killers, a pair, perhaps a couple of men who were close friends. People who worked together or spent a lot of time together. That led him to his list and it got shorter. He could eliminate men who worked alone, cab drivers and delivery men.

On the other hand, there were the EMT units, Fire Departments and even Police that were night people and could often pick up young single women. Some bartenders always worked in pairs. There were also the people who worked the Emergency Reception areas of local Hospitals. In this area where the bodies were found there was only one hospital.

As he walked back to his car, he heard the higher siren if

an EMT unit going to some call. That reminded him that the killers needed some additional important items. First, they needed an area where they took the victim to and played out the first part of the game. That meant a bed and all the BDSM toys, some were expensive.

They needed an area where they could clean up and dress and paint the body. That meant a tub or shower and a lot of make-up and even perhaps some clothes stored somewhere. Finally, they needed some way to move the body from their location to the presentation site. That last part was important, because they had done this again and again and no one saw anything unusual.

Sitting down in the car, he decided that last part had to be the one that would trip them up. He needed to go back and interview, no just talk to everyone who was in the area of each death. It was tedious but it was part of the job and you never could believe what you found out by listening.

CHAPTER FIFTEEN

Starting out the next night, he didn't go into the office, but went direct to the first location and since it was early in the night there were lots of people out and looking for entertainment.

It didn't take long to get the bum on the corner to talk. A ten in his small bucket and he would talk all night. All he saw were cops, big cars with lights, an EMT unit and more cops. This was the same type if information he got from the apartment dweller, those who would talk. Most claimed they saw nothing, heard nothing and who only read about the murder in the papers.

The ladies in the sex shop were friendlier and he even got a cup of coffee with cream, but the story was the same. No one saw any one toting a body down the side street. There were no unusual vehicles in the area and they all saw the many flashing lights. One girl did say that a local EMT unit parked about two blocks over, waiting for calls. She said it was probably one that had answered the call the night of the murder, but she wasn't sure as she hid in the dressing room in back.

He ate a meal a few blocks away at an all night greasy joint and made notes in the small computer, checking for any personal calls from the office. Most of the calls were not important, but Jean had sent him some closeup photos of bruises that showed up after removal of all the make-up.

The next night he was able to visit two of the sites of the death scenes. Both of these were no longer blocked or marked off. One did have some faded chalk lines, but the weather and traffic had erased the memory of CSI's methods. The girls had never left a trace on the cold cement.

The story was the same from everyone. Nobody saw anything or anyone. The answers were that there was no unusual noise and no unknowns lurking around. In fact, the strange reports that he made a note of was that everything seemed too quiet. There was the mention of the EMT that was in the area and the fire department showed up with their own emergency unit at these two, but not at the others.

On a hunch, Damian ran an official text through his Chief to data information for the ID's of the number on the EMT units, Fire Departments, and first police detachment that showed up at each scene. It would take them a couple of hours to get back, so he found another all night diner to rest and eat.

Before he was done the first report came in on the Police Car numbers identification. That was easy as everything was logged and even tracked by GPS. There were no matches. There was a different first responder of the cops from the closest location. Damian decided he could strike cops from his list of buddy killers.

Getting back on the street, he listened and watched as the night passed and the streets had less traffic. He was again on a side street with fog coming in from the river. No matter how far away you got from the docks, winter or summer, the damp in the air was part of the night on these alleys.

With his fedora keeping his head dry, the street lights were only white blurs above, throwing down some light but more shadows. He had passed a door that was open with some cartons outside but no one in sight. The inside light also did not help light up the street full of litter and trash.

He was coming up to the corner of the main street that was not any cleaner or brighter. But on the corner was a business where he was going to enter to ask all the girls about the death scene. He had some ways to break through their hesitations and lies.

The door would be open as Damian knew in this city, such places without signs, didn't close their doors, even in the heat of summer or freeze of winter. Lucky for everyone that the river kept this city at a livable temperature most of the year. One of the things he had to get across to these women was that he was really here to protect them along with the people that lived up on the mansions on the hills.

Crime was blind and was a virus that would strike where the opportunity was available. The pros in these shops made money, and some on the street wanted whatever the ladies had tucked away in their stockings.

Coming around the corner that was almost all shadow, the double door was open on both sides and a woman was standing in it. She was a silhouette, back lit by the red in the room. She had her long legs apart in very high heels that even in her dark out line accentuated her leg muscles. It also showed that she had very little else on and was a very lush figure.

If the madame had asked the lady to step into the doorway, it was smart advertising. The lady stepped back as he moved into her space and waved an arm of welcome. Before she could talk, Damian pulled up the bottom of his jacket and flashed the badge. That stopped her welcome and words except for a loud call over her shoulder.

"Beatrice, cops." With that she moved across the room and took a chair with a couple of other girls.

From the back came a woman who looked like she could be an attorney. She was dressed in a suit and comfortable but stylish shoes. She also didn't look afraid or disturbed. So, she probably had paid her under the counter dues to the local precinct.

"A policeman?" She asked in a quiet manner.

He unbuttoned the jacket, more to be comfortable, but to

also show the gold shield.

"Oh, welcome Detective. Can we be of some help?" Beatrice held her hands together in front and stood calmly. He was beginning to get a good vibe from this lady.

"I am doing investigation on the murder of the girl that happened around the corner from here. I am looking for some back details and maybe something that was missed the first time through. Everything will be kept confidential." He put a little emphasis on the last word.

"Well, unfortunately for us and good for you, you picked a quiet night. How do you want to start?" She looked over her shoulder as if she was going to suggest a private room.

"First, I need to talk to anyone that was here the night of the incident. It would be fine if we do it as a group if there are several who are available." He raised his eyebrows under the brim of his hat indicating it was up to her how to handle the next move.

"Well, Detective, let's move into the next room while I send one of my girls for my laptop." She nodded at a girl who got up and took off as she moved toward the inner door. Damian followed closely and they soon turned to the left and went into another room.

It was still a sex shop room with red velvet drapes and low lights, but there were lots of long sofas and a large low round coffee table in the middle.

Beatrice took a seat and opened the laptop and soon began to call out names sharply. With the names, women began to show up at the doorway and entered to take a seat. Evidently, everyone was listening somewhere close by. There were two names that no one answered when called.

"Detective, these ladies were here the night the poor body was found." Now Beatrice looked around and sat her computer away from her on the low table. "Sorry, but a couple are missing tonight."

From where he leaned against one of the velvet walls, Damian took his hat off and held it between his hands, to roll the brim back and forth. He glanced up over at each woman with a large smile.

"No problem. This is just a conversation for everyone to talk about what they were doing when they were interrupted by the sirens or yells." He watched as most of the girls shifted in their seats, some near others and no one said anything.

Now holding the fedora in one hand, he twisted and pointed to a woman across the room. "I would guess that such a beautiful woman like you were entertaining a customer and was interrupted by all the excitement, right?"

There were some giggles, and the woman he addressed smiled as she shook her head. "No, I was finished and counting my cash. But I did hear some feet running down the side street before all the uproar."

"I was asleep." Another girl stated and now everyone was talking. Words flew back and forth and then he heard what he needed.

Someone mentioned about the sirens and about the cops and the fact that the EMT unit that was in the neighborhood. There it was again. Something that was tied into all the murder scenes.

Staying long enough to thank Beatrice and say goodbye to all the girls, the tall Detective finally made it back to his car, ready to call it a night. He did a quick check on the computer to find he had a message from the data nerd. The guy was really good. He had the fact that only one EMT unit had appeared at each murder scene. The guy provided Damian with the unit's number and station location.

Walker decided after a long sleep he had a place to visit. He had refused all the offers from the ladies, promising to come back on another night.

That time off, in his dark apartment with the heavy drapes,

Damian had dreams of dark eyes and cream colored skin. He woke in a sweat and had to wonder if he would ever need to take a vacation to Canada.

At last, he gave up on the rest of his sleep and got up to shower and went out to find a place that served breakfast late in the evenings. He did go by the office to drop off a report to the Chief, mainly because he had some time to delay before going over to the EMT station.

Parking across the well lit street, the garage or station reminded the Detective of a small fire department unit. It had large doors on both ends that were open to each street and many of the red and white vehicles were parked inside.

There were two facing him on this street, probably ready to roll out on a call. He felt there would also be two more by the other door to run on the other street. Whatever was needed and however many depending on the emergency call.

Along one side was a simple office and then a long work area with lots of counters and one truck with its hood open. No one was working on it so perhaps the mechanics only worked daytime. On the other side was a couple of simple tables and chairs with some people in uniforms sitting. There were also a couple of doors that probably led into the area for beds and a cafeteria.

Leaving the hat in the car and his coat open so the shield was prevalent, Damian approached the man sitting in the small office. It was mostly open and allowed him to start talking as soon as he approached.

Deciding to start the conversation, Damian nodded. "Slow night?"

"Thank goodness. We don't have many of them. What can I do for you, Detective?" The man at least recognized the color of the shield.

"I have an easy one for you. I'm stuck with talking to everyone about some older investigations. My data people tell me that one of your units was called to most of the incidents. I have to talk to the people who were on that unit at the time of each event. Boring work for me but someone has to do it to complete the reports." Damian leaned in on the high counter where the man worked.

As happened with people who had monotonous night jobs, Walker made a sympathetic friend and soon had the names of the two men who were assigned to EMT Unit 1221. He even had their general assignment area.

CHAPTER SIXTEEN

Steven Hardy was in the system because as a EMT registered driver he had his fingerprints on file. But he had no record, not even traffic tickets that would show up in the last five years. He was registered at 5′11″ and 200 pounds. Damian believed that at almost six feet tall, the man probably was solid muscle in that kind of weight.

The assigned partner was James R. Manchester, but Jimmy had a record. Working on the EMT truck he had taken extensive Medical and Emergency courses and passed them with flying colors. Perhaps he was trying to turn his life around. In his police file at 5′4″ and weighing 160 pounds at times, he was a skinny man who made his sexual preference for men obvious.

His arrests had been for misdemeanors mostly, a DUI, drug use and drug selling. His longest incarceration was for one year. But for the last couple of years, he had been clear.

Because of their positions, their photos were included in the file. Hardy had light hair and was what the ladies would call handsome. Even though Manchester had some good looks about him, he looked like a nerd or a wimp. There was the bit of a silly smile in his arrest photos.

Could these two be the serial killers of several innocent women? It would take a lot of proof to find that answer. First out of pure interest, he wanted to meet the duo personally.

It only took him a little over an hour to find the EMT Unit 1221 parked on a side street next to the curb. It was in the normal expected area assigned, although it could also have returned to the station house. This unit preferred to remain active and on the streets.

As the low Charger drove by, Damian could see that the front driver's portion was lit with Hardy sitting behind the wheel. He was comfortable with his feet up on the dash and was working on a clip board. The back was also lit, but since there were no windows he could not see if Manchester was back there. There was just a reflective light seen through in front and a slight amount from a crack of the slightly opened back doors.

Needing to talk to them under conditions that would not arise suspicions, he went back to the office and under the bright lights began to put together the investigation report. He was careful to make it coherent and fill in the forms that would help as he followed up on what some would call a hunch. He needed to substantiate the reasons and clues and facts for following up on the history of two men for the last few months. He wanted to dot the i's and cross the t's and go beyond. He had a feeling that he had found the killers, but those beyond him didn't want to know about his feelings. They wanted hard proof.

People outside the police department would never understand the amount of reports and length of forms that had to be filed by everyone from the blues who walked the streets, the guys on intake desks for different positions and all the way up to the Commander in Chief. Even with electronics, so called paperwork and reports filled a few hours of each shift for anyone who wore a badge.

Feeling like he had covered everything, including his own ass, Walker began to try to find a way to talk to the two suspects without alarming them the first time. There had to be a time when they returned to the station for normal overhaul of the truck or even supplies for medical.

That time when he was off duty, he slept well in his dark

apartment. It took Walker a couple of nights of watching his suspects and the Unit when they made a trip to answer a call of a car crash. It involved several cars and another EMT also was called out with several Ambulances. All of them ended up taking injured to the local hospital.

Taking extra coffee with him, Damian went over to the EMT station and gave the guy stuck behind the work area the cup.

"Hey, thanks. I remember you. You work the night shift too. I would think that once you get the gold shield you would get to pick days all the time?" The guy laughed as he took a sip of the hot drink.

"You looking for another unit? I don't remember what one you wanted before, but I have everything right here." Now the guy wanted to be friends.

"You know how it goes." Damian tipped his own cup. "The boss wants to know where the units get their supplies. I suppose he thinks they steal them from the local box stores."

Now they both laughed, with the worker's being genuine and Walker's trying to only join in. Now the man pointed out the second door across the way.

"We, or me and my day partner check out the inventory weekly and turn in a report. Everything is in there and the Units can pull what they need." Now he leaned back and enjoyed the coffee as if that solved all the inventory problems.

"So, the guys on the units go in there and pull what they need. How do you keep them honest? How do you know how much they have pulled?" Walker was done with his creamy coffee and moved over to throw the cup into a large waste container.

"Oh, here is a unit now that will need to resupply. Wait around and I will show you the trick.

The EMT truck, all in white and red stripes, pulled in and two men got out in the standard uniforms. One was a big handsome guy who was dirty and smiling and soon was high fiving with some of the people at the tables. He went into the door after yelling for his buddy. The other man who was on the truck came out the back, leaving the doors wide open. He was a small thin man and wasn't near as messed up as his partner. In fact, he was wiping his hands on a white rag as he climbed down the two steps from the opening. Unlike his buddy, he didn't speak, but only nodded at the group sitting around. He also went into the door that led to an area where they probably could get showers and a change of uniforms.

Not in any hurry, Darian took some time to talk to his new friend. "So how long have you worked here?"

It was not unusual for a bored late night worker to be glad to spill the beans to anyone that would listen and pass the time. After all, he didn't have much to do until the people went for supplies or a special call came in or a truck needed to be kept in for mechanical checkup.

Within a short time the small guy came out, clean and in a new uniform. He went to the other door and came out with some supplies he took to the back of the unit.

Now the new friend smiled and turned a computer screen towards Damian. On it was a list of some items.

"All the supplies come to us with a stamped bar code. The door scans them in and out. We get the info right here. No one gets anything out that the door doesn't report." The man was proud of his more than modern tech.

On the other hand, Damian knew that what one genius created another found a way around it. He had arrested a lot of smart crooks. As Damian admired the equipment, Hardy came out of the rest area and approached the Admin. desk.

"Hey, Mika. How's it going tonight?" This muscular handsome man was always friendly.

"Hi, Steve. I see you guys need a lot of supplies. I guess you were caught up in that big mess. Hey, this is a friend,

Detective Walker." Now Damian turned and nodded at his first suspect.

"Yes," Damian held out his hand. "I think I have seen your unit at several of the cases where I was called out. You and your buddy get around in the same area."

The big EMT guy did shake without unusual pressure and a short grip, letting go as he turned to Mika. "We got our supplies. Let me sign and we need to get out of here. Nice to meet you Detective." With these words Damian was dismissed as Hardy did the proper paper work and turned with a wave. Manchester never did show his face again as he was busy in the back of the truck. Probably putting supplies away.

"I gotta go, too. See ya." With that and his first impression of his two suspects, Walker got back to his car. His next goal was to get into their personal residences. But when he pulled their info back up on the favorite little computer, to his surprise, the two men lived together.

While that made things easier for him, and since they were at work, he drove over to the address and parked a block away. The interesting part was that it was quite a drive away from their place of work. It took an hour and a half late at night and in traffic during the day it would be a longer drive.

The location was an old neighborhood with three and four story buildings that were narrow and butted up against each other. Basically, due to the age and smaller size of the buildings, people or families could lease a whole floor or sometimes the complete building. There were even cases were some of the buildings were owned by families.

Hardy and Manchester leased the second floor of a building that had an expansive two car garage on the first floor. The third floor was rented by someone else for strictly storage. The public lease record did not record what was stored on the third floor except it met code. He had checked and found that Manchester drove a fairly new SUV and Hardy rode a Harley. He thought the rides fit the two people he had seen for a short time at the EMT station house. He also found it interesting that they had a home in a busy city that still gave them a lot of privacy.

Not wanting to be obvious, he left his hat in the car, but changed in special soft shoes and put on his favorite leather gloves. He took a couple of special tools with him, including an unusual flashlight. Making a trip around the block, Damian was comfortable that a lone man walking on the dark streets in this neighborhood didn't draw any attention. In fact, he only saw one other person who had a dog at a curb who ignored him. This also allowed Damion to check out the back entrance. But his choice was the front door.

Coming up to the short entrance to the driveways and walk to the doorway beside the garage entrance, he walked up at a normal pace but without hesitation. To his relief, this first door was not locked. Like many people, this is where deliveries and mail could be dropped off out of the weather.

There was a door to go to the garage and the stairs that let up to the apartments. It was a wide stairway and when he got to the second floor there was a large balcony with plenty of room for the door and entrance to the apartment on that floor. Everything was well lit and as he looked around, he could even see the extra emergency bundles in corners.

Pulling one of the gadgets he had appropriated from an arrest about a year ago he opened a tool and inserted it into the keyhole. Pressing a button, there was a soft buzz as the tool began to expand different small flanges, filling what was expected in the lock. When the buzz quit, Damian turned the key and the lock opened. It was an automatic lock pick. A marvelous little toy.

Before opening the door, Damian slipped a tight stretch cap over his head. He didn't want to leave a hair for DNA when he did an illegal search. He had the gloves on that would allow him to pick up a dime from a floor, but leave no trace. His soft shoes left no imprints on carpets or wood and tile floors. As a cop he had learned from those he put in jail.

Turning the flash on at shoulder height, he could see the living room was pretty standard for two guys. The furniture was comfortable and the TV was huge. There was workout equipment in one corner and plants with flowers in another. The open kitchen was immaculate, but had a lot of lacy hot pads and many recipes on the fridge.

He went down the hallway to the bedrooms and bath and there the story was so different.

Chapter Seventeen

The door on the left, taking up the area behind the kitchen, was a very large immaculate bathroom. The glow from his flash was reflected everywhere. Yep, this had to be the results of Manchester.

The first door on the right was a large bedroom suitable for any man. It was in dark woods with a king size bed in the middle and a couple of old but solid chests on each wall. The end wall was open and showed a double closet. Did they both use this room?

The last room held only a bed. At this time, he would not do a deep inspection as he did not want to warn them that they were under suspicion. But he needed to find something to confirm his own hunch that these two men were the serial killers. He stepped into the room and switched the light onto a different mode.

The flashlight was not the bright small police issued. It was small and bright, but it could be adjusted and it would light up an entire city block. Damian didn't need that much, but he wanted this room that had no windows to be lit up for him to see all the details.

There was a very tall chair against the wall across from the foot of the bed. Also, there were several small cameras attached high up on the walls. The bed was of heavy metal with a large decorative metal headboard of bars and a footboard to match. The bed was made neatly with pillows and everything covered and tucked under a dark brown duvet. There was a stand on each side at the head of the bead that was nothing but legs and no drawers. The light over head had larger bulbs and the original cover had been removed. It was meant to light up the entire room.

It all seemed too strange and then he saw the tools. Hanging down below the edge of the cover that didn't reach the floor at the end of the bed could be seen and open unhooked cuff and a bit of a chain. Letting his eyes follow the path of the hem of the duvet, there at the front, down below a pillow was a reflection of a chain.

Moving into the room and up to the pillow, Damian lifted the cover slowly and the whole device, chain connected to the metal headboard and the wrist cuff. Being extremely careful to replace the cover to the same position, he stood for a moment.

In his mind he saw one of the innocent girls across this bed. He saw her fear and pain and the pleading in her eyes as she struggled behind the ball gag. The cuffs on her wrists and ankles didn't cause the pain, it was that she was stretched so tight and far that her muscles screamed. The confusion inside her mind was compounded by something cold and too large stuffed cruelly into her rectum. Why didn't he stop? What else did he want? Tears had made her hair wet, but that seemed to please him.

Shaking his head, Damian let the evil vision fade away. He had to find a way to stop this pair. Just in this room he had found enough to convince him he had found the right men to confirm his hunch. Now he had to find the proof. He needed traces of them around the women, and DNA at the scenes, and facts that they had brought the women to this room.

On the way out he moved inside the bathroom. He didn't want to touch or disturb anything as he believed the Manchester probably was compulsive about having things in their place. But with his thin gloves, he opened cabinets and found a treasure of supplies. In the one large standing cabinet they could open a ladies beauty salon. On one shelf alone he could see dozens of red nail polish, all in straight rows.

In the medicine cabinet were so many bottles of meds, there was no room for razors or toothpaste. From what he could see, without touching any of the pill containers, they were issued by different doctors and prescribed to Manchester.

Finding as much information as he could without leaving a trace of being in the apartment, he moved towards the front door. He glanced at a table by the door and the mail which of course was divided and systematically laid out, there were no bills. So how did these two pay their debts, through the Internet or by their bank?

The lock clicked in place behind him and he went up to the third floor to inspect the landing. Damian was really looking for any security cameras or something that would notify the owners of visitors. He pulled out his cell phone and checked for service and it was clear.

Keeping his phone open and in his hand, he went down the stairs and out of the building. Taking his time, he walked or better strolled the way back to his car. Damian even leaned against the low front fender and made a call to the data nerd. The guy didn't have any more for him so he took the time to thank the guy for his time and work. It never hurt to have friends in unusual places. Plus he was making sure he was not attracting attention or being followed.

Comfortable that he was alone and only another late guy going home, he decided that was a good idea. The soft purr of the big engine brought contentment as he tooled the Charger slowly out into the foggy streets and headed home.

For the next few shifts, he would be watching his suspects, showing up at each of their emergency calls. He knew they would soon get on to him, but he hoped being careful knowing the police were watching would save a woman's life.

In the meantime, he had two friends doing deep investigation. He had Jean in the morgue looking again at the two bodies of the last two murders. He asked her to check for marks of the nipple clamps and possible deep cuts that could be identified to a particular fastener. He had his nerd checking with the FBI records to see if nail polish or make up could be identified and traced back to original products. It was now boiling down to tedious police and forensic work.

There was a car crash that EMT Unit 1221 answered the notice and Detective Walker also showed up to help make a report. That was the only emergency that night. The next two nights the team of that particular truck were off duty. The truck was left in the garage for a standard check and oil and fuel.

Even though it was not a week-end, the team had to work five shifts with two off, as there always had to be teams working on the busy week-ends. Deciding that these two men were like him and worked all night, that even on their off time, they would live a night life.

While he ate his breakfast at an all night restaurant at the start of his shift, Damian had time to think. What did two working men do on what was their so called Saturday night off? He went out to check on his suspects and follow them to find out.

Sitting down the block in the low dark Charger that hid itself in the shadows, the Detective looked at the car's clock as Manchester came out and walked down the street to the all night corner bodega. When he came out a half hour later, it didn't look like he had purchased food, instead Walker could see the shape and advertisements of cleaning supplies. This guy was a true neat freak.

It was almost two hours later when one of the garage doors went up and the large Harley came roaring out. The mighty engine in the car found it easy to follow the fast two wheeled beast.

Hardy was going to a special club and Walker recognized it as they both pulled into the enclosed parking log. The name of the club was On Top and Walker needed to change from his long coat to a black leather jacket. He left his hat in the car and knew he only needed an attitude to get inside.

At the entrance there was a reception area with a beautiful woman with very few clothes behind a counter. On one side stood a very large muscle bound man in a tuxedo jacket and no pants. He didn't speak but she gave a great smile as she welcomed Damian.

"Member or Visitor, sir?" she asked in the mode of a submissive. But she had someone's collar on her neck so she was protected.

Taking a Dom mode which meant being rude, Walker looked at the draped doorway. "Visitor. Just a short trip." Acting in the way an acknowledged Dom would, he ignored these two and moved on through the drapes. This led through a short hall that opened into the first standard room for a BDSM party. There was a bar on his right and a couple of tables on the left. Then on beyond were the first scenes.

He decided to go to the bar and get a strong drink. The one thing he wasn't worried about was Hardy recognizing him. It was dark and the few lights were either red or flashing at odd times. He was going to have a hard time finding his guy in this crowd. Moving in between a couple of chairs, he chose to stand and order whiskey straight. He had worked this scene a few times and even tried it out for a friend. It wasn't his stick. He knew all the rules and that everyone said it was consensual. But he also saw some bodies in the morgue that had not submitted and had been miss-used by this idea of unusual and sometimes painful sex.

Then towards the back of the room there were some cheers. Out of curiosity, he carried his drink and wandered through the half-naked and so many people in unusual bits and pieces of clothes, to where some people were watching a scene.

Steve Hardy was under a spotlight and Walker had to admit the Dom knew how to display himself. Most of the Masters in this place were in leather with straps across their bodies and over their chests with tall pointed boots.

But Steve had his muscular tanned body naked to the low slung very tight faded levies that hung almost to his lower hair line. He also had on his motorcycle boots and the lights reflected off the chains that wrapped around the thick soles and high heavy heels. Everyone in this room had to wonder at one time or another what he did with those chains, including Damian.

There was a naked man kneeling before Hardy with a towel in his hand, but he was not covering himself. He obviously had a hard on and was bursting to release, but Hardy was saying something. Hardy had a soft whip and as he stood straight, he smiled down at the man and with a quick flip of his arm he brought the whip over the man's back and buttocks. With a groan the man hunched over with the towel in his lap and everyone knew he was ejecting into the cloth. His moans were both of pain and pleasure.

At last Steve took a heel in front of the beaten male, laid the whip down and took the man's head in both hands. He tipped the guy's crying head up and put a full deep lasting kiss to the submissive. There was applause and the spotlight went out.

Now Walker had additional information to think about. Hardy was bi-sexual. Walker felt right down to his own solid shoes that Manchester was not the one to rape the girls. So Hardy went both ways.

Giving his half finished drink to a standing sub, Walker left the club and felt like he needed to go home and take a shower. But once back in his, there were some hours before sunrise and it was only another night on the job. He drove to the back of Station 12 and parked in one of the forbidden spots.

CHAPTER EIGHTEEN

Going on up to the Detectives wing, he took a seat at his desk and went through his messages first. He had some pink slips that he tossed away, but he had important ones. The first one he called back was to the data nerd about tracing nail polish and make-up.

"Well, Detective, I have some interesting information. I have bad news and maybe a possibility." The guy seemed like he was really into this investigation.

"Go ahead and lay it all out for me." Damian leaned back and put a foot up on the edge of the shelf of his unit that held the terminal and all his folders and a keyboard.

"Well first of all the manufacturers of nail polish make each color in large quantities when they are producing a color. They mix a large amount in vats and then begin to ship containers out to bottling plants and from there the bottles are packaged in loads of 24 in a case and shipped literally all over the world.

The FBI records state it is possible to tie a bottle to a manufacturer, but not to an individual except for fingerprints on the bottle. The process is almost identical for all types of make-up including lipstick."

When the enthusiastic nerd quit for a breath, all Damian could say was, "Damn."

"But," the date pro continued. "Let's talk about one item and use it as an example for all the other items. Nail polish. If the suspect still has the same bottle and has used it on one woman or more. What the FBI does is pour what is left out on a flat sterile surface and hunt for skin cells or DNA that was picked up by the brush as it is used and dipped back in the bottle. I think you probably got the idea."

Now Damian sat up and smiled. "My data friend, I think I love you."

Disconnecting the office phone, while he was on a high, he made one more call from another pink slip.

"Jean, how's it hanging?"

"Well, if it isn't my handsome Detective." The Pathologist gave a chuckle and he could almost see he pretty smile through the phone. She was a good looking woman in her late forties.

Chuckling, Damian asked a pertinent question. "You got something for me?"

"Yes. Your hunch was on spot. One of the nipple clips is crooked and when it bites it leaves an unusual deep mark that is rare and not found in others. I got good photos and imprints from both bodies on different side breasts. If you find those clamps, someone is going up for a very long time." Now there was no laughter in her voice. Jean had handled a lot of murders and the deaths and unusual treatment of these girls were getting to her.

"Thanks, Jean. Get copies of all that you have to me and my chief and the Prosecution's department. My next job is daytime and involves a warrant for a search and double arrest.

When you are a night person, there are a few times that you don't mind getting up in the morning. There was that time when you looked in the mirror to be sure there were no razor marks from the close shave and that the dark tie had the proper sharp knot.

Getting into regular polished shoes could even be accepted under some circumstances. Today Detective Damian Walker was wearing a standard suit and leaving all weapons behind. It was a day he was looking forward to as he went downstairs to get into his car. But he didn't take a route to Station 12. He was heading to the city's main Courthouse.

In that large grand old building, five stories tall with the eagle on top under the USA flag. It had six large columns in front with the proper large wide stairway leading to the second or main floor.

The Detective parked in the underground lot that held too many cars, but he put his Police notice in his window and parked in a particular place marked off for Officials. It was near one of the elevators. He had made this trip two other times.

From the time the two men had been arrested until the jury brought back a guilty verdict, almost two years had passed. Their team of lawyers led by a beautiful woman had done everything to delay, postpone and keep their clients free. Fortunately, thanks to forensics, pathology reports, law enforcement producing camera videos and first person confirmations, they were done.

Today Detective Damian Walker would stand in the back of the court room and hear them sentenced to death for all the murders. As he got off the elevator and walked down the wide busy marble hall, he decided that afterwards he needed a nap. Yes, and then later he had an invitation to visit a special lady at a particular red door.

Yep, it would be another foggy night and time to walk his streets and watch.

The End.

About the Author

M. Garnet, author of over 80 novels, is known by her friends and fans as Muriel Garnet Yantiss, so you will find her on Facebook under that name. But her website is under her author's name at www.mgarnet.com. M. Garnet has written for many years and has many books on a cross-genre, but all seem to be Happy Ever After. She admits she had a special like for SciFi since reading Dune so many years ago.

Her own long and exciting life adds details to her stories that bring a complete and interesting process that gives the reader some education that they might not have known about before reading her books. The inside workings of foundries, the fact of diamond mining on Inuit territory in Canada, and best of all that, we already found a way to talk instantly from point to point to break Einstein's theory on Faster than Light.

As an active member of the local chapter of Florida West Coast Writers, she was the 2019 Book Challenge Coordinator for the group. She has been a long-time member of the NAPW and has done presentations and short articles for years. M. Garnet enjoys her membership in Science Fiction & Fantasy Writers of America.

Her writing has won her many awards and reviews. These include the 2017 Golden Heart, 2017 Rita, 2016 Sexy Scribbles, 2016 Passionate Ink, 2016 Shelf Best Indie Book, 2015 National Novel Writing Month Winner, along with top reviews on many of her Novels.

www.ingramcontent.com/pod-product-compliance
Lightning Source LLC
LaVergne TN
LVHW012333100826
845148LV00017B/2280

* 9 7 8 1 4 8 7 4 4 1 5 6 2 *